Samuel S Boggs

Eighteen Months a Prisoner under the Rebel Flag

A Condensed Pen-Picture of Belle Isle, Danville, Andersonville....

Samuel S Boggs

Eighteen Months a Prisoner under the Rebel Flag
A Condensed Pen-Picture of Belle Isle, Danville, Andersonville....

ISBN/EAN: 9783337081270

Printed in Europe, USA, Canada, Australia, Japan

Cover: Foto ©Andreas Hilbeck / pixelio.de

More available books at **www.hansebooks.com**

EIGHTEEN MONTHS A PRISONER

REBEL FLAG,

A CONDENSED PEN-PICTURE OF

BELLE ISLE, DANVILLE, ANDERSONVILLE,
CHARLESTON, FLORENCE AND
LIBBY PRISONS

—— FROM ——

ACTUAL EXPERIENCE.

S. S. BOGGS,

Late Sergeant 21st Illinois Infantry,

AUTHOR AND PUBLISHER,

LOVINGTON, ILLS.

1887.

INTRODUCTORY.

Recently, seeing by the statistics of ex-Prisoners' Associations that there are of all those who were released from the Southern prison hells only twenty per cent. now living, and, fully realizing that in a few years more the last one of us will have passed away,—it occurred to me that it is our duty to ourselves and to. the memory of those who have been exchanged to another world, that we, as far as possible, each leave a pen picture of at least the mildest part of our prison life. Of course, we know that it will not do to portray those prisons in all their horrors, lest we destroy the credit of the whole story; hence, we must hold back much of the worst part. People who did not experience what the inmates of those Rebel prisons did can not believe it possible that such brutality and barbarism could have been practiced in civilization, forgetting that slavery clouded the conscience and calloused the hearts of our cruel keepers, whose notoriety for cruelty as slave-drivers gained their appointments as prison-keepers, where they could satisfy their barbarous appetites on helpless captives who possessed no property ue. Cruel men are always cowards, who in time of war seek places re they can revel in cruelty and gore, with but little danger of y to hemselves. The Confederate government, with no regard s honor, sought out this class of demons as the keepers and of its helpless captives, and never in one instance did the chief executive of the Confederacy show any disposition to substitute humane keepers for the demons in charge, though he was fully aware of the true condition of the prisons from the reports of his inspectors and the petitions of many of the best people of the South. I know that the darkest parts of the memory of those terrible prisons will pass into the forgotten when the last survivors tongues are hushed. Some accounts have been written, among which is that very excellent history by Comrade John McElroy, which all true patriots should read, as it is truthful and authentic. I am well aware that those who endorsed the barbarous treatment of Union prisoners now try to smother the recital of those wrongs.

With charity and forgiveness for all who ask it, I will now take the reader of this pamphlet through nearly eighteen months under the Rebel flag; and with as few unvarnished words as possible I will unroll the panorama as it appeared to your friend and well-wisher,

Samuel S. Boggs,

Late Sergeant Co. E, 21st Ill. Inf't.

Lovington, Ills.

CHAPTER I.

At the outbreak of the Great Rebellion in 1861 I was twenty-one years old, and just starting out in life for myself. I was a stout, healthy youth, just passing into the first flush of manhood, and scarce knew what an ache or pain was.

In the latter part of April news came that Fort Sumpter had been fired on, and that Rebels were seizing government forts and property, and seemed determined to destroy the Union. In the Northern States the situation had been hotly and thoroughly discussed; while in the South free speech was not allowed and the common people were led to believe their rights and property would be taken from them by the Abolitionists of the free States. The cunning leaders of Secession took advantage of the excitement and swept those misguided men into an army to overthrow the best government the sun ever shone upon. The rank and file of the Rebel army had taken but little part in the political trickery of the Secession leaders; they were honest and fair-minded, and ready to resent with their lives any indignity offered them, or their country.

In the North the people were divided: the loyal Democrats and Republicans wanted the Union saved, while the Copperhead element worked with money and sympathy to help the Rebels destroy it. Thus the cyclone of Rebellion threatened to sweep Fair Columbia from the list of Nations. The insulting blow had been given and the government called for help. I, with a number of other young men of my neighborhood, bade farewell to our homes and prospects of education and business and enlisted in what turned out to be the 21st Illinois Volunteer Infantry, with Ulysses S. Grant as its colonel. We marched into the enemy's country, taking part in many of the battles and exciting scenes of a soldier's life from '61 to the fall of '63, which brings us up to the battle of Chickamauga, the general details of which I leave you to learn from the histories of the Great Rebellion.

It was about noon. The Rebels made a desperate charge; there was a crashing roar; the air seemed full of bullets, dust and Rebel yells. Men went down on all sides of me; we were in a hand-to-hand encounter; some of our men had saved themselves by timely flight, but our retreat was cut off; it was either surrender, or foolishly throw our lives away.

We were quickly disarmed and hurried to the rear of the Confederate army, and closely guarded. More prisoners were brought in until about nine hundred were gathered on the banks of the Chickamauga creek. We were then marched ten or twelve miles, put on board of some freight cars, and run to Atlanta, Ga., where they turned us into large slave pen. A table was brought in, a blank book, a bottle of ink and a pen, were placed upon it; then, a Rebel major called out, "*Attention, Yanks!*" If thar's a-r-y sargant among you all, what kin write, I want him to come and write you all's names in that ere book." One of our sergeants went to the table and suggested that each man be allowed to write his own name; then it would be more likely that the names would be spelled correctly. The major said, "All right." The men wrote their names, and as they did so, were turned through a narrow gate into another pen. The major watched the writing until twenty-five or thirty had signed the roll, when he said: "Well, I'le swah, you-all's got book l-arnin'; " one of the guards called to a citizen on the fence, saying: "*Oh, Mastah Hunt*, we's kotched a hull passel of school-marstahs; they kin *all rite, by gosh!*" I signed the roll, and passed through the narrow gate. Two guards (or Rebels) seized me, took my knife, hat, blanket and shoes; this was done quickly, and I was ordered to keep quiet and go to the further end of the pen, where some guards had my stripped comrades herded in a corner like a flock of shorn sheep; some had lost all but their shirts and drawers; they skinned us of all the clothes that were not too much worn; then put us on a freight train, gave us some corn-bread, when we were started for Richmond, the capital of the Confederacy. After a three or four days' run, we arrived at the James river, opposite Richmond about ten o'clock at night: crossed to Bell Island on a bridge, passed down some steps, and through an iron rolling mill, where all was aglow with hot iron; George Baker, who was just ahead of me, said to me: "Sam, here is the iron works, and hell is next." He was about right, for Bell Island was one of the Rebels hells. We were forced to an open part of the island, where a shallow ditch inclosed about six acres of ground, the earth from this ditch being thrown outward, forming a low bank on which walked the guards; we were ordered into a spot not occupied, and told to lie down, and keep down, or the guards would shoot us.

The wind was blowing a frosty gale from down the James river; where we lay was as open and exposed as any sand bar. Not a tent or shelter of any kind, and without fire; having fasted all day, we were hungry, cold and miserable in the extreme; some had neither pants, coats, nor blankets, and we huddled in bunches like shivering swine, covering ourselves with the pieces of tents and rags left us at Atlanta.

We were men who had passed several years of soldier life, had often slept on the cold wet ground, in our rain-soaked clothes, but this was a few degrees worse than we had ever experienced; here, we dare not get on our feet and move around. Some of our boys were suffering from inflamed and undressed gun-shot wounds; the pain from which forced groans from their fevered lips; we were powerless to help them, and could not even give them a drink of water. Although the James River was within a few yards of us, it would be certain death to try to get to it.

About nine o'clock next morning we were counted for rations, and a piece of unsalted corn-bread, about the size of a half-brick given to each man; we were then allowed to get water from the river. There were a number of prisoners on another part of the island, who were principally captured at Gettysburg; they had been prisoners several months, and were a set of ragged, lousy, skeletons; part of them had some ragged tents, the balance had no shelter. We were kept on the island several days, then taken over the river to the city of Richmond. The officers and severely wounded men, were separated from us, when we were taken to the infamous Libby Prison, where our name, company and regiment were taken, then sent from there to the Smith building, a four story brick, with bare walls and floor; we located ourselves in the building, and began to talk over the situation. Some of us had been secretly warned as we were leaving Bell Island, that our money and all valuables would be taken from us in Richmond. So far no such attempt had been made. We hid our money in shoe soles, buttons and in any manner we thought would outwit the Rebels. While we were thus engaged the door opened, a low-browed, cruel-looking Rebel officer came in, followed by a slave bearing a table and blank-book o' his head. The officer called out: *"Attention, prisoners! form in li double file."* We formed. Some guards were stationed in front ·. rear of us, and we were ordered not to move or talk.

The officer then said: "I am Major Turner, provost marshal of the city of Richmond, *Confederate States of America* I am under instructions from *my* government to have you surrender to me your money and valuables. Your name, company and regiment will be carefully entered in this book, and when you are exchanged or paroled, it will all be returned to you; for which I pledge the honor of the Confederate government. I now give you this opportunity to save your money and when I am through taking that which you surrender, you will be searched by men who are experts, and all they find will be confiscated.

One of our men asked permission to ask a question; it was granted. The comrade said: " Major Turner, inasmuch as you are acting in this matter for the Confederate government, will you, as its agent, give us receipts of that government for our money?"

"No, sir; I am not here to fool my time away; I am ready to receive the valuables."

Considerable money was given up.   The searching gang came in (and they understood their calling).   The money put in brass buttons was lost.   They tried the buttons with the jaws of a knife; if the button did not mash it was cut off the coat.   They found considerable money, but some was so well secreted that it was not found.   One man put several bills in some tobacco leaves, and was chewing it; when they searched his mouth he carelessly dropped the tobacco in his hand until the examination was made.

It is needless to say, that we never had returned to us any of the ~y we gave up.   Here, as on the Island, we got the half-brick-,~.l piece of corn bread once a day, with a small allowance of buggy soup, made from stock peas, and occasionally some meat of horrible carriony flavor.   We were told that it was mule meat, and were certain from the roundness of the rib, that it was not beef.   As the days and weeks passed away, we lost flesh rapidly; some were dying with lung 'ever, and some from sheer starvation.   Here we had plenty of water, there being a hydrant on each floor.   About this time, our government learning that the Rebels were keeping us almost naked and starving in unwar ~ buildings, and in the unsheltered place on Bell Island, asked through the exchange commissioner, that it be allowed to furnish provi sion, clothes and medicines, to be given to the Union prisoners; to which the Rebels agreed.   About fifteen tons of supplies were sent through the lines by flag of truce boat.   A small portion of this was given to the prisoners, the balance was sent *direct to the Rebel army, ordered there by Jefferson Davis and his cabinet*, the records of which are n existence to-day.

Through the bad faith of the Rebels the exchange of prisoners had stopped. General Grant paroled and turned loose twelve thousand Confederates at Vicksburg. They were immediately armed and sent to Lee's army. When an exchange of prisoners was to be made our government wanted twelve thousand to off-set the men that Grant paroled this the Rebels refused to grant. Other causes then arose whic stopped the parole and exchange of prisoners. Our government could not, with honor and safety, exchange on the terms offered by the enemy.

The Rebels now seemed determined to starve and torture us, with the intention of raising such a clamor in the North, that our government would be compelled to accede to their dishonorable terms, and to so cripple and disable us that when they did get their terms we would be unfit for soldiers.

About that time the Richmond papers stated that the stench from the prisons was endangering the health of the city; and that it would be well to move these "*Lincoln hirelings,* to where scant fare and cold weather would reduce them according to the laws of nature." Consequently we were sent to Danville, Va.

We arrived at Danville about the 10th of December; here they had converted a number of large brick buildings or tobacco factories into prisons. About five hundred of us were put in what was known as prison No. 5, near which was a large store-room, where the citizens of the surrounding country hauled their tithes, or tax in kind, being one-tenth of all farm products, which they were compelled to pay to the Rebel government.

A large amount of cabbage and garden truck centered to this store. The Rebels hunted out the coopers from the prisons, and set them to making barrels, and a large number of slaves cut the cabbage into kraut for the Rebel army. The leaves and stems of the cabbage, raw, and well seasoned; spiced with worms, cabbage lice and tobacco spittle, were given us as dessert, and we were glad to get it, as it did not lessen our other rations.

We would gather around the pile of refuse as it lay on the floor of our prison, and imitating cattle and sheep, bellow, blat, and paw the floor, etc., impatient for our share of the fodder. With the addition of the cabbage leaves, and a little bacon (or, instead, a raw sweet-potato), our rations were much better here than at Richmond. We suffered much for water, however.

Each mess of ten was allowed to send one man with a pail with the water squad, which would be sent, under guard, once each day to the Dan river, about thirty rods distant; we sent our strongest man for the water. Should he fall from weakness, or other causes, and spill the water, we did without that day. During the month of January, lung-fever and small-pox were claiming their victims. At one time there were eighty-six cases of small pox in our building; many were sick from other causes. Some days no water or rations came in, on account of the fear the Rebels had of catching the disease. At such times, our fever-stricken comrades suffered terribly; the Rebels evidently had an elephant on their hands, and were afraid of him. They became less vigilant, thinking, perhaps, we were too much afflicted to attempt to escape. Some of us worked a hole through the floor, and commenced digging a tunnel, putting the dirt in an old cellar, and digging with a cooper's addz and a door hinge. In about three weeks' time we had a tunnel 147 feet long, passing under the guard line, a high board fence

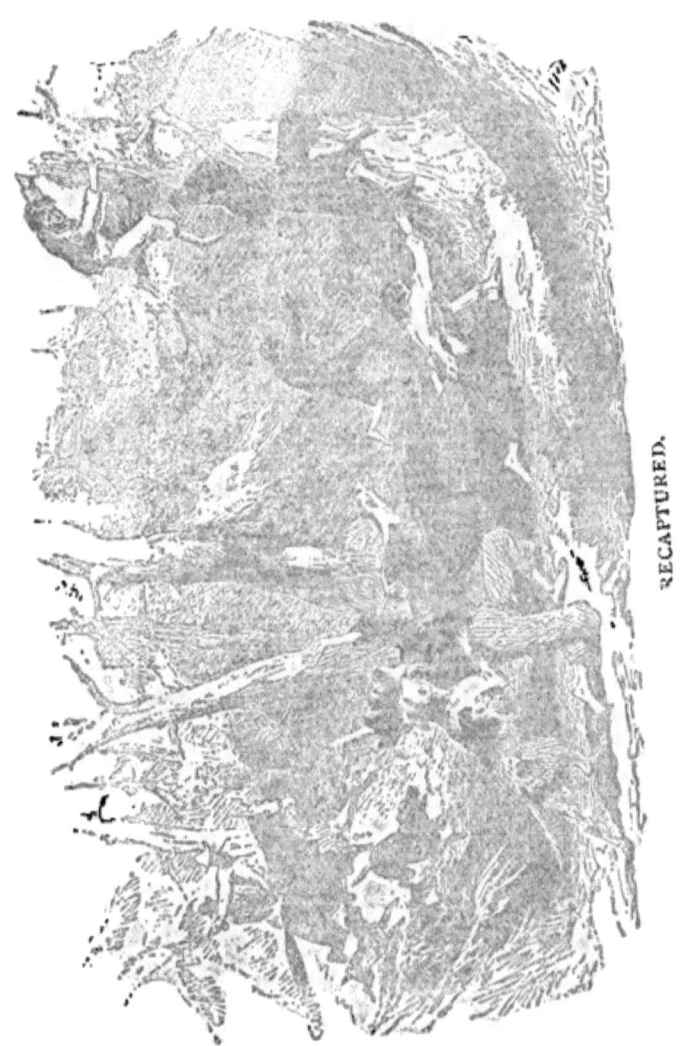

RECAPTURED.

d ending under a colored family's house. Eighty-six escaped. When was discovered it was midnight; the town was alive with excitement; ins were fired, and bells rung. The exciting news was sent far into e country, that the "small-pox Yanks" were loose and scattered over ie land. Men with dogs and guns were sent in every direction to atrol the country. Inside of ten days nearly all had either been killed r recaptured. Many died in the woods from exposure; being in the evered stage when they left the prison.

The night the tunnel was finished and opened shoes were taken rom the unburied dead and from the living who could not travel or did iot know of the tunnel, which had been secretly made. These were iund of great service in running through the green-briar and black-ierry bushes. We dare not keep in the roads or paths, but, scattering, nade our way through the woods and thickets, each choosing his own oute, wading or swimming streams, hiding in thickets or fodder stacks hrough the day. It was about the middle of February; the nights vere dark and rainy, and sometimes snowing. My scant clothing and flesh torn with briars, and not knowing what was ten feet ahead, made it extremely difficult to make much headway toward reaching our lines, two hundred miles away. The bloodhounds found my trail and I was soon run down and sent back to the same prison, where I remained until in March, when we were told that an exchange had been agreed upon, and we would be sent to our lines. Next morning we were ordered on board of a freight train, and started north. There were several reasons for believing that we were going to God's country; then "the hollow eye grew bright and the poor heart almost gay, as we thought of seeing home and friends once more." When we got to

Petersburg we were put on another train and every precaution take
to keep us from escaping. The train started south, for what point w
could not tell. Our train groaned and creaked along for five or si.
days. After adventures of wrecks, escapes and recaptures, we arrive.
at Macon, Ga. From Macon we turned nearly south, over a railroac
passing through a continuous stretch of dense pine woods and vine
tangled, black swamps. After a run of about sixty miles we stoppec
in a clearing where there were some seven or eight houses—all made
of logs, and the roof-boards held to their places by poles being laid
on them. We learned that this was Andersonville. We were taken
from the cars to an open piece of ground just east of the station
looking east about a quarter of a mile, we could see an immense
stockade. The last few days of our journey we had no water, and
were suffering from thirst. The car that I was in had been used as a
lime car, and had a half-inch of lime dust on the floor when they loaded
us in at Petersburg; they put about seventy-five men in each car; an)
moving around would stir up this dust. Our lips and 'tongues seemed
parched and cracked. Two died in our car on the trip. There was a
small brook within two rods of us; the guard line was between us and
the water. I was pleading with the guard to let us to the water, when
a little grinny-faced Rebel captain, on a sway-backed gray horse, rode
up and shook a revolver in my face and said: "You Got tam Yankee!
you youst vait, und you got so much vater vot you drown in booty
quick!" He rode around us several times, bouncing high in his
saddle, flourishing a revolver and swearing at the guards and us alter.
nately. After satisfying himself that we did not have anything worth
robbing us of he proceeded to form us into nineties and detachments.

: of our sergeants was put over each ninety, and one over each achment. By this time we learned that this was Captain Wirz, the nmander of the interior of the prison.

We were ordered forward toward the big stockade, moving quietly l painfully along, our spirits almost crushed within us, urged on by : double file of guards on either side of our column of ragged, lousy :letons, who scarce had strength to run away if given the opportunity. e neared the wall of great squared logs and the massive wooden gates it were to shut out hope and life from nearly all of us forever. The cheerful sight, near the gate, of a pile of ghastly dead—the eyes of iich shone with a stony glitter, the faces black with a smoky grime, id pinched with pain and hunger, the long matted hair and almost .:shless frame swarming with lice—gave us some idea that a like fate waited us on the inside. The Rebels knowing our desperation, used .ery precaution to prevent a break; the artillerymen stood with myard in hand at their canister-shotted guns, which were trained to weep the gates. All being ready, the huge bolts were drawn, the gate wung open on its massive iron hinges, and as we moved into that hell n earth we felt that we were cut off from the world and completely at he mercy of our cruel keepers.

The creek which ran through the pen was pointed out to us. A ush was made for it, as we were famishing from thirst. The water soon became cloudy; two comrades, to get the clear water just above the "dead-line," and, not knowing the danger, reached beyond it, and both dropped dead in the water, shot by the guards on the wall. We dared not move their bodies until ordered to do so by a Rebel officer, who was some time in getting around. The water running red with our

comrades' blood, stopped the drinking until the bodies were remov '
We had not been in the stockade ten minutes until two of our num.
were ready to be put on the dead pile we had seen just outs
the gate but the poor fellows missed the horrible torture which v
planned for them and us, and which if I knew I had to pass throt
again I would cross the "dead-line" and ask the guard to show
mercy by tearing my body through with the ball and buckshot fr
his old Queen Anne musket.

CHAPTER II.

The Confederate government, through the agency of Howell
Cobb and John H. Winder, designed and built the Andersonville
stockade, where it would not be subject to raids from our armies, and
evidently with the design of destroying its captives with natural
agencies, viz.: slow starvation and exposing them, unsheltered and
uncared for, to the burning sun, the rains, fogs and deadly miasma from
the quaking, slimy quagmire which occupied over three acres through
the central part of the pen. It has been shown, by Confederate
evidence, too, that there were many good sites near by, with good
springs, and much better in every respect than the site chosen, and I
have never heard any excuse given by Davis or his agents for enclosing
this death-dealing swamp in the prison.

The dense pine timber was cleared away by cutting the trees in lengths of twenty-five feet and hewing them as large square as the logs would permit. A trench five feet deep was dug around seventeen acres of ground; the logs were then set on end in this, close together, forming a wall twenty feet high; each stock being spiked to a horizontal timber three feet below the top of the wall, on the outside. The pen was longest north and south, sloping from either end to the quagmire, through which ran the little creek, about four feet wide and five inches deep, it forming the water supply for the prison; at regular intervals were the guard-stands, forty-four in number, and placed near the top of the wall, where the guards could overlook all parts of the prison.

There were but two gates, both on the west side, about ten rods from either corner of the pen, and called the North and South Gates; inside the wall and twenty feet from it was the "dead-line," marked out by strips of pine board supported on stakes three feet high. This the prisoners must not touch, nor go beyond under pain of death. Around the stockade, and at suitable distance, were a number of earthworks or forts, built up sufficiently high so the artillery could sweep the pen with shell and grape-shot. About twenty rods south west from the south gate, on high ground, overlooking the prison, was the large log-house wherein quartered the Rebel officers. The Confederate flag floated from a pole in front of this house. Near this pole were two cannon, or signal guns, used to warn the whole Rebel force in case the prisoners attempt to break out. At various places between this house and the south gate were the different instruments of torture, viz.: the stocks, thumb-screws, barbed-iron collar, shackles, balls-and-chains, etc. There were three kinds of stocks—one in which the prisoner stood on his tip-toes, his hands fastened over a piece of timber,

REBEL CAPTAIN WIRZ MAKING HIS DAILY VISIT TO THE BLOODHOUND CARS. THE BIG DOGS SPOT AND ZERO.

(From O'Dea's picture of Andersonville.)

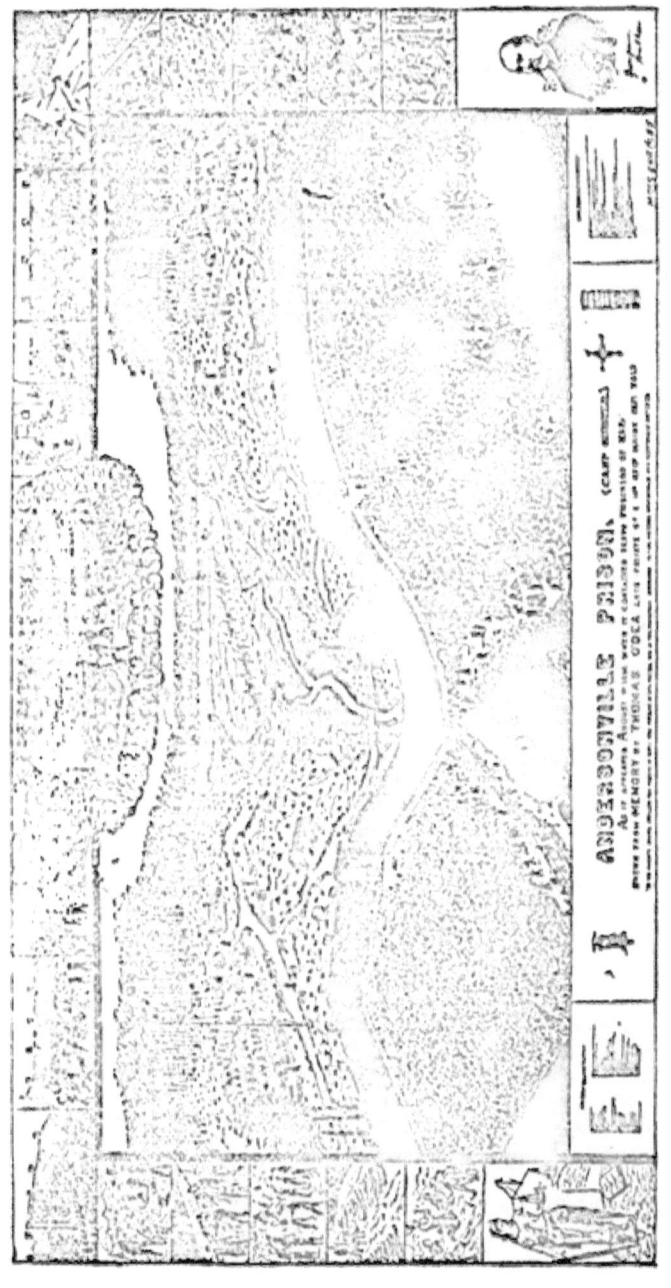

ANDERSONVILLE PRISON, (CAMP SUMTER.)

under which his head is crowded forward; another timber forces the small of the back forward. In the second stocks the prisoner sits on the ground, with hands and feet elevated, and fastened to a frame-work in front of him. The third stocks was a horizontal frame, the prisoner lying on his back, with hands and feet fastened, the head being fixed in an extending head-board, which is moved outward until the body and limbs are in a painful tension. These instruments of torture were brought from where they had evidently been used to hold slaves in obedience. Our prison-keepers seemed to handle them with familiarity. About a half mile northwest from the pen is a large sandy field, where the dead were carted, and packed in trenches without box, coffin, or clothes, and but a scant covering of earth. On the road to th potter's field was a log house where the dogs and bloodhounds we kept—some thirty or forty in number; these were used to patrol the the surrounding woods and run down escaped prisoners and runaway slaves. The small creek which ran through the prison from west to east, came from numerous spring branches near the prison, along which were the tented camps of the Rebels and a large number of slaves,—the drainage from these camps and sinks, passing into the creek. Just outside of the prison wall was a large cook-house operated right on the creek bank. Combine its slops with the sewage of the Rebel camps, and the water was about as pure as the washings from a slaughter house. Outside of and around the stockade were numerous piles of pine knots, from which bright fires were kept burning dark and foggy nights to light up the surroundings.

The spot of ground we were to occupy was pointed out to the sergeant of our detachment, who guided us to near the northeast corner of the pen, where we arranged in rows, north and south, leaving a narrow alley between each ninety. We then commenced fixing our bedding-place, or, rather "spooning-ground." There was yet some debris left from cutting and hewing the palisade timbers. The prisoners who had been there, some of them more than a month, had consumed nearly all of the refuse for fuel, making huts and "dug-outs." Some, with a view of speculation, had stored by many of the best poles and sticks. However, there were yet some small poles and sticks to be had along the edge of the swamp; with these, and sun-dried bricks, we made a temporary shelter, which would do in dry weather, but when it rained it seemed to rain more in the hut than it did outside, and our ick generally had to be made anew.

Our rations now consisted of a pint of coarse corn-meal and about a gill of *stock* peas per day.

After we had done the best we could for ourselves and sick comrades (of which there were quite a number), some of us went among the earlier arrivals to see if we could find any of our acquaintances (there were about two thousand prisoners in the pen when we came in). We found some of our friends who had been confined in Richmond and on Bell Island; many were suffering from frost-bite, their toes and fingers rotting off. They had experienced extreme cold, being on the Island all winter, without shelter and but little clothing. The James river had frozen over three different times so teams crossed back and forth on the ice. Many of the boys had perished on the island, and a number had died here; but the change had improved many, as they had more room, fuel and shelter. They were all anxious to know if there was any exchange news. We could give them none except how we had been deceived when we left Danville. They had been disappointed the same way when they left Richmond and Bell Island.

Time dragged slowly by, and we felt utterly God-forsaken and beyond the limits of civilization. While our praying bands petitioned the Almighty to soften the hearts of our cruel keepers, the kind hearted Southern people were petitioning Jefferson Davis to remove Winder and Wirz, and put humane keepers in their places; but relief came not.

We tried to occupy our time in bettering our shelter and killing the lice, which had gotten a good start of us while we were being moved. When the sun shone out warm, we would take off our rags, and sitting along in a row, our hands soon were in motion, which would lead a distant observer to believe that we were having a knitting frolic, in which he might not be mistaken, as "nits" were part of the game we were after.

Prisoners now arrived by train loads day and night, the Rebels emptying the other prisons into this place. At this time there were about seven thousand in the pen; among the late arrivals from Richmond, were about one hundred roughs, who were graduates in crime and vice, from the pits of sin in New York City. These men were professional bounty-jumpers, who had enlisted as substitutes for large pay. Through the vigilance of the recruiting officers they had no chance to escape, being sent to the front, where they took the first opportunity to give themselves up as prisoners, expecting to be paroled and turned loose; being disappointed in this, they secretly banded themselves together, with cut-throat obligations to rob, and, if need be, to murder their fellow-prisoners. We learned from other men, who had been confined with them at Richmond, that they were a thieving set. They

located on some high ground on the south side of the creek. Having some money, and better supplied in every way than the other prisoners (which was perhaps due to their thieving qualities), they spliced their tent stuff together, and getting some poles (from those who had them for sale), made what they called a "big sheebang," which afterward became known as "Raider headquarters." They courted favors from the Rebel officers, for which they volunteered to act as spies, to give information as to the doings of the other prisoners. They would appear kind and very sociable with the new prisoners, and help them locate and at the same time find out if they had anything worth stealing or murdering them for.

Each detachment and ninety was counted by a Rebel sergeant every morning at eight o'clock, and about the middle of the afternoon a four-mule team drove in with a wagon-body full of coarse, chaffy corn-meal. The sergeant would call for two men from each ninety to draw rations; then the man who had a pair of pants or drawers, which could be made to hold meal by tying the legs at the bottom, loaned them to the sergeant for the consideration of a spoonful of meal. The rations would be drawn in proportion to the number found in each ninety— then carried to their respective grounds, divided out, each man getting for a day's allowance, nearly a pint of the meal, a tablespoonful of peas, or, instead, about one ounce of beef; a piece of bone weighing six or eight ounces, being considered equal to an allowance of beef. Nearly all would eat their rations as soon as issued. Many for want of means to cook them, would eat their rations raw. In all my eighteen months' prison experience, the Rebels never furnished us one item in the way of cups, cooking vessels or clothing (except water pails at Danville, Va).

Some of the prisoners, when captured, had a fruit can with wire bale, hung on their belt, and a tin plate, or half-canteen, and a worn case-knife in their haversack.   These they were generally allowed to keep, and their value to the prisoner can hardly be estimated.   Experience taught us to pick up any scraps of tin, hoop-iron, etc.   On our way to Andersonville, our train wrecked and I rolled up some tin which had been torn from a car-roof, my messmates secured some spikes and broken bolts, these we smuggled into the prison among our rags and pieces of shelter tents.   With the assistance of a tinner, and using the bolts and spikes for tools, we made a tin pail, which would hold about four quarts and a square pan about four inches deep, and holding about six quarts.   In this we cooked our rations, and sitting modestly around the pan, would clean it out and wish for more.   When w loaned our pan to neighboring messes it would generally be returned with a spoonful of mush, as rent.   Some who had no way of cooking, would go around with a bunch of meal, about the size of a common turnip, done up in a dirty rag, calling out, " *Who wants to trade cooked meal for raw!* " and by offering a large per cent. they generally got a trade.

The Rebels, though watching and searching closely for money watches and jewelry, did not get it all by direct robbery.   Some of prisoners came in without being robbed.   It depended a great deal c what officers were on duty at the time the prisoners arrived.   If they arrived in day time, and Hume or Duncan were on duty, the prisoners lost everything worth having.   The Confederate soldiers who did the fighting at the front, seldom ever robbed their captives.   My experience was that they were well meaning, humane and honorable, and would divide their drink and rations with their prisoners.   They honestly believed they were fighting for their rights. Of them I have no word of complaint to offer.

Considerable money found its way into the prisons. Perhaps one man in two hundred would have from one to a hundred dollars. One dollar in greenback was worth seven in Confederate. A traffic sprang up between the Rebel soldiers and the prisoners; some of the prisoners were taken out to work, building a cook house, and doing various other jobs. They would be guarded or else would be on parole of honor; they were turned in at night and taken out in the morning. We used them as the medium of exchange. The Rebel quarter-master, with an eye to business, put up a shanty about the middle of the north half of the prison, and appointing two of our Jay Goulds—Charley Huckelby and a Beverly—put them in charge of it. He then supplied them on commission with meal, peas, salt, sweet-potatoes, tobacco and any article which it was thought would draw hidden money from the Yanks. We called this the suttler shop; its goods were sold at incredible prices; a teaspoon (moderately rounded) full of salt, 25 cents; a small biscuit 50 cents in greenback, and other goods in proportion. The famished skeletons, or more like mummies, would stand around and look in on good things, then consult their money, then their stomach s, and the ney was handed over.

No one not there in person can form anything like a correct idea of our appearance about this time. We had nearly all been prisoners from seven to nine months; our clothes were worn out, a number being entirely naked. Some would have a ragged shirt and no pants, and some had pants and no shirt; another with a soldier cap on his head, and not another stitch on him; their flesh wasted away, leav-

THE TRAILING HOUND.

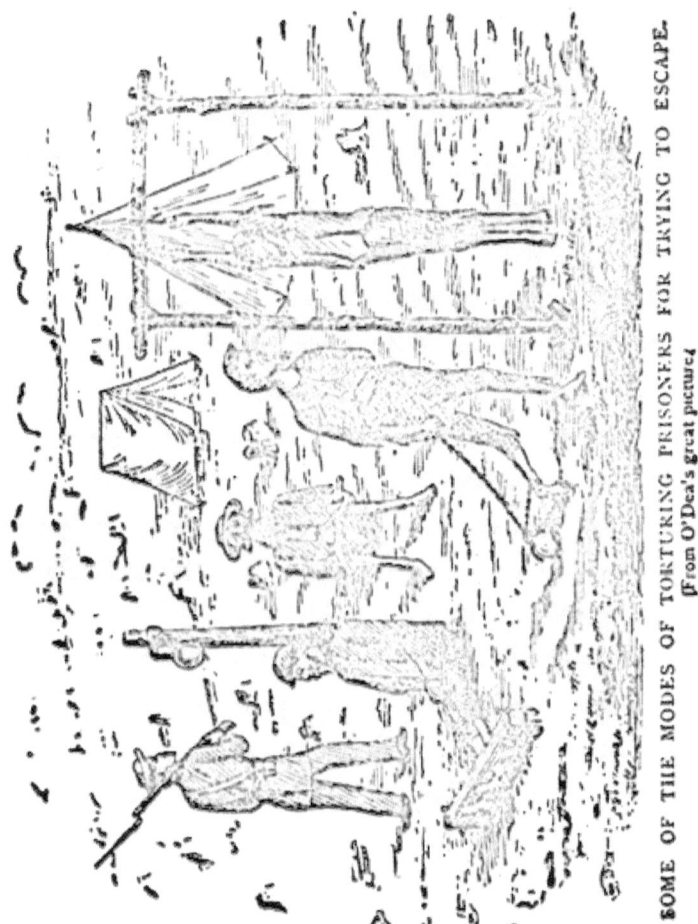

SOME OF THE MODES OF TORTURING PRISONERS FOR TRYING TO ESCAPE.

(From O'Dea's great picture.)

ing; the chaffy weather-beaten skin drawn tight over the bones; the hip bones and shoulders standing out so a hat could be hung on them; the faces, and exposed parts of the body coated to the thickness of paper with a smirky black soot, from the dense black smoke of pitch pine we had hovered over since we had been in Andersonville; our long matted hair was stiff and black with the same substance, which water alone would have on effect on, and soap was not to be had. I will not attempt to describe the condition of the sick and dying, who could now be seen on every hand. The "dead-line" was claiming its victims, and the stocks and various instruments of torture were being patronized. The deep-toned baying of the blood hounds breaks the morning stillness of the forest and swamp; some poor fellow has got beyond the guards and is being chased down; the sound of the hounds dies away; instead we hear the far-away tooting of a horn, the listening Rebels cheer; the runaway is caught; in time they appear with him. He is led bleeding, and torn to the stocks, fastened in the infernal machine; the maggot flies deposit their eggs in his wounds. He is punished for ten or twelve hours, and then turned into the prison with wounds uncared for. A few days later we see him a working mass of maggots.

Many plans had been tried to escape, such as tunneling and scaling the walls on dark foggy nights, being carried out for dead, and hanging under the ration wagon, etc. Nearly all had been failures on account of traitors among us; just who the traitors were we could not tell. Some thought the New York roughs were the ones, others spotted a one legged, hook-nosed man of the 38th Illinois. He had been outside several times, and seemed to be on intimate terms with Captain Wirz.

About a hundred men were working a tunnel. It started in a mud hut near the "dead-line;" a Rebel officer and some guards came in, broke in the tunnel and took the occupants of the dug-out to the stocks and chain-gang. The traitor must now be found; evidence accumulated against "Hook-Nose;" the enraged prisoners got after him; he ran or hopped to the dead line, and crawled under the railing; the guard leveled his gun and ordered him to get back. He straightened up against the inside of the "bead-line," pulled his shirt open, and told the guard to shoot, saying: "If I have lost the confidence of my comrades I want to die." The guard fired, the buck-shot and ball, tearing away the lower jaw, and entering the lower part of the neck. There were two regiments guarding us; the 26th Alabama and 55th Georgia. The Alabamians were intelligent and kind-hearted, and would not shoot a prisoner unless he was trying to escape or disobeying orders. The Georgians were ignorant and brutal, and seemed to delight in shooting and torturing the prisoners. It was a 26th Alabamian who shot Hubbard, the one-legged man just spoken of, for which he was not to blame. Hubbard violated orders in crossing the "dead-line," and refused to go back when ordered. Had it been a 55th Georgian he would not have been warned, but shot down without a word.

The Alabamians would talk to us from their posts, while the Georgians were liable to shoot if we spoke to them. There were some other Rebel troops garrisoned here, but I do not know what regiments. There were in the pen about two hundred colored soldiers of the 8th U. S. Regulars, captured at Oolustee, Fla., in March; there were a number of them wounded. One fellow had a hand shot off, and some enraged brutes had cut off his ears and nose, and otherwise mutilated him. The doctors refused to dress his wounds, or even amputate his shattered arm; he was naked in the prison, and finally died from his numerous wounds. The negroes were put in a squad by themselves, and a white union sergeant appointed over them. They would be taken outside, and made do work. One day a 55th Georgian, without word or act of provocation, put his gun to the sergeant's breast and fired, murdering him instantly, simply because he was in command of the negroes.

It was now about the last of April, and about 11 per cent. of the prisoners had died during the month. There were over ten thousand in the pen. The ground was all taken up, except along the borders of the swamp, where the human filth was from three to ten inches deep, and from the frequent rains, had become liquid, and flowed out over the quagmire, where it fermented like yeast. Millions and millions of flies swarmed over it, and this mass of putrescent filth, became a lake of rolling, squirming maggots. "The largest would crawl out on the hot sand, shed their tail-like appendage; wings would unfold, and an attempt made to fly; and thousands were clumsily dropping all over the camp. They tumbled into our mush, bedding-places and on the faces of the sick and dying."

We thought the pen was as full as it would bear, without crowding, but one morning we found about two thousand well-dressed, clean, fat-looking young fellows occupying one of the main streets. The camp was all excitement to hear from the North and learn how the war was progressing. We gathered around them, but they acted as if they wanted to keep us as far away from them as possible, and seemed so perfectly dazed by the surroundings that but few of them would talk.

In time we learned that they had been captured at Plymouth, N. C., where they had bravely held out against vastly superior numbers, and finally had to surrender. "But," said one of our boys, " how did you manage to get in here with your knapsacks, blankets and all your outfit? Didn't the 'Old Dutchman' and his assistants rob you?" "Well, I will tell you," said the Plymouth boy, " we had heard how ' Old Jeff' was robbing and starving his prisoners, and, thinking we had better let them kill us than to be robbed of everything, we would not surrender until they had promised that our personal property should not be taken from us; but had we any idea that this place is like it is, darned if we wouldn't have all died right there, for it is certain death here anyway. My God! this is hell, isn't it?" These Plymouth boys were nearly all young men, from the best families of New York and New England; they had been on garrison duty along the sea-coast, and had received many visits and luxuries from loving ones at home. They had not become inured to hardships like the soldiers who had experienced long marches and slept tentless on the cold wet ground. They had served out their three years, just reinlisted and received their veteran bounty and back-pay; consequently had brought about fifty thousand dollars into the prison. This money soon began to move, large prices were paid for ground room, wishing to keep their men together as much as possible, to better protect themselves from the "Raiders," who were now adding to the horrors of the nights by their murders and robberies. For a consideration the old prisoners would move and scatter to other spots. The money they got for this real estate would be changed for Confederate money and invested in the sutler-shop. Thus little shops were started all over camp, and soon did a thriving business. Those who had money could buy, but they who did not have could stand back and look wishfully on. The merchant was always armed with a stout club to defend his wares.

All kinds of gambling and confidence games were started. The Plymouth boys brought in knives, watches and some small kits of tinkers' tools. These were brought into use and workers of metal, carvers of wood, bone, etc., were busy making trinkets, which found ready sale among the Rebel soldiers. The main street was lined on either side with the busy traders. "Might was law, with no one in authority." The "Raiders" were increasing in numbers as the rascally-inclined joined them; they were organized and divided into bands, under the leadership of some experienced thief or "pirate." They were known as the "Curtis Raiders," Delaney's Raiders," "Collin's Raiders." etc.—some six or eight bands in all—all under the chieftain-ship of William Collins. The "Raiders" were growing fat from their plunder, while many in the pen were starving to death.

CHAPTER III.

Prisoners Arriving by Train-Loads. — Eight Thousand Sick. — Rations, Quantity and Quality Smaller and Poorer. — Howell Cobb Incites the Guards to Murder the Prisoners. — Prisoners Asked to Join the Rebels. — A Few Take the Oath. — Corn-Bread-Fruit-Cake. — Horrors of the Night. — Death Rapidly Doing Its Work. — Thieves and Robbers. — Arrest and Hanging of Six "Raiders." — Wirz Scared; He Orders the Artillery to Fire into the Pen with Grape and Canister. — We Lose Our Corn Crop. — As Our Number Increases the Rations Decrease. — Winder Boasts that He is Killing More "Yanks" than 20 of Lee's Regiments. — His Orders to Murder the Prisoners. — Winder is Promoted by Jeff Davis as a Reward for His Cruelty to Prisoners. — Jeff Davis Responsible for the Wanton Destruction of Life in Southern Prisons.

There were now desperate battles being fought all along the line of our advancing army, and large numbers of our men were being brought in as prisoners. They came pouring into our pen at all hours of the day and night. We thought when there were ten thousand in the pen that it was crowded to the last degree; but now it contained eighteen thousand. The space between the "dug-outs" and little tents was packed full. At this time the pen contained at least eight thousand sick and scurvy-rotted young men who could not stand on their feet. The rations had diminished in quantity and quality from day to day, and the last roots of the stumps dug from the ground for fuel. Earth was taken from the higher ground and the filth, along the edge of the swamp, partly covered, and the new ground occupied to the very edge of the swamp. The net was being drawn tighter around us; the Rebels built another strong wall about one hundred and twenty feet from the inner wall; more artillery ranged on the prison and the punishment was more severe for trying to escape. The 26th Alabama and 55th Georgia had been sent to fight Sherman, and some eight or ten thousand Georgia reserves took their places. These were nearly all ignorant boys, who had never been away from home, and knew but little about the war, except what they had heard in the fiery speeches of the Rebel leaders, from which they were led to believe us only a set of monstrous cut-throats and thieves, who deserved the most horrible death, and that they would be doing a God's mercy to the world to kill as many of us as they could. They went on duty, and on the most frivolous pretext would shoot a prisoner. The murders at the "dead-line" were of so common occurrence that we took little notice of them; but these murderous boys became tired of their grim sport; the terrible stench of the prison was making them sick; they wanted to go home, and a number of them deserted. Captain Wirz telegraphed Howell Cobb at Macon to send him more men for guards; all his available forces were at Atlanta fighting Sherman. Cobb came down in person; the Confederates formed a square around him; he stood under a shady tree on some high ground not far from the prison, and made a fiery speech of a half-hour's duration, appealing to them, as the future hope of Georgia, asked if they would turn "this horde of Lincoln's brutes and hirelings loose upon the sacred soil of Georgia?—this band of assassins who had cost the lives of so many of your fathers and brothers; to put them where you can hold them, and thus help your bleeding country's cause? Turn them loose, and how long would your property and your mothers and sisters be safe?" He implored them to do their duty, obey their officers and the prison commander. *The murders along the "dead-line" increased.* The prison was crowded to its very edge, and it was impossible to keep from getting near the "dead-line;" there were hundreds of crazy men in the pen, who, in spite of our watching, would get to the "dead-line," and many sane men would calmly fold their arms and step across it to end their misery. The guards in shooting these men nearly always wounded or killed some one who was not near the "dead-line;" the bullet would pass through the body of the man it was intended for and, glancing on through the pen, would find a lodging place in some innocent man's body. The number shot in this way could be counted by scores; we were constantly in as much danger of being shot here as at the battle-front.

Rebels came in nearly every day, trying to get mechanics to take the non-combatant's oath and work in their shops; the oath was to never bear arms, or to assist directly or indirectly, in any military operations against the Confederate States of America, and obligated us to work in such places as that government might direct. This was the same thing, or worse, than going into the Rebel army, for we would take the places of men who were then doing the work, and they would be compelled to go into the ranks. The only men caught on this hook were a few of the "Raider" gang; the balance seemed determined to honor the old flag, which they had sacrificed so much to save. Wirz was now issuing corn-bread to about half of the prisoners; a large cook-house had been built, in which this corn-bread was made. Here was a large long box, in which was soured corn-dough sticking to its sides and bottom, over which swarmed millions of flies, a wagon-load of meal was scooped into this box, burying flies and gnats; water was dipped from the filthy branch to wet this meal, then stirred with pole

DIVIDING OUR RATIONS OF CORN BREAD.
(From O'Dea's picture.)

and shoveled into large pans, marked off in half-brick sizes, and when baked sent into the pen, and a half-brick-shaped piece given to each man on the north side of the creek. The next day the north side got dry meal while the south side got the baked bread, and so on alternately. This bread was made of yellow meal, and somewhat resembled fruit-cake, the flies taking the place of the raisins, etc. Nearly all the old prisoners now had scurvy; the gums turned black, swelling beyond the teeth and pouching out the cheek; the teeth became loose and dropped out. They were picked up and put back with the vain endeavor to save them;" the mouth became cancerous and the patient lingered and died. In others the limbs turned black and swelled to the greatest capacity of the skin ; black, watery sores opened, gangrene set in, and death shortly followed. The whole prison was a hell of torture and insanity. You could hear praying, groaning, the laugh of the lunatic, and the curse which is the dying farewell of hope. The sun grows hotter, "Raiders" bolder, the guards more murderous, stocks more terrible; the chain-gangs were full of victims and the ground swarmed with lice. As the long scorching day closes and the air grows cooler, we lay on the unsheltered filthy ground trying to shut out with sleep some of the surrounding horrors. Millions upon millions of mosquitoes come from the surrounding swamp to feast on our emaciated bodies; their buzzing hum added to the bedlam of the prison—with the hooting of the owls and the mournful notes of the whippoorwills—howled a requiem broken only by the crack of the muskets of the murderous guards, or the sound of their voices as they cry out the hour of the night from their perches on the palisades. I have lain on the battle-field in the solemn hours of night surrounded with the dead and dying, heard the piteous, agonizing cries of the wounded, but it was nothing to compare to this den of misery and woe, the memory of which will be ever present with those who experienced it.

We entered into a secret plot to dig tunnels and undermine the inner wall, force the stockade, storm the forts and rifle-pits, and strike for freedom. We failed on account of the traitors among us. The plot was discovered and the leaders put to torture. There seemed to be no relief; we must rot in this living grave. Over half of the old prisoners were dead, and nearly all of those living prostrated with scurvy and gangrene. The dead carts were now hauling a hundred a day to the trenches in the sandy field. There was a place outside where some of the sick were taken, but they were so poisoned by the foul stench of the prison that nearly all died. Unless one was there t is impossible for the mind to grasp the magnitude of this hell on earth. There were now nearly thirty thousand young men—*young men* who had been pronounced sound and healthy, and the best material in the land where they had come from. *Thirty thousand young men!* More than you could find in many of the States—cooped up in the narrow confines of twelve acres, starving, drinking and breathing poison for months.

The " Raiders" were having everything their own way. It was a common thing to find dead men in the morning, with throats cut or heads crushed in. The small traders seemed to be their favorite game. By this time (about the 1st of July) the " Raiders" got so bold that bands of them went in daylight and robbed by wholesale. If a man tried to defend his goods he was knocked down and robbed. The Rebels made no effort to remedy this. Something must be done. A

WE HANG SIX OF OUR OWN MEN.

burial squad (our own men) to mark on a stake, at the trench, the location of each body. There was quite a traffic done in carrying out these dead men (or stiffs, as they were called). The trinkets, and keepsakes, which had found their way into prison, and the brass button with the eagle stamped on it, were highly prized by the ignorant young Georgians, who had no idea of the American eagle as an emblem of liberty. They would be at the gates with sticks of wood, twists of tobacco, or a cowhorn full of soft-soap, ready to trade with the prisoners who were carrying out the dead. We have just come out with a dead man, and watching the little wicket, that opens through the large gate, we see two live skeletons coming out, carrying a dead skeleton, which, perhaps, would weigh sixty pounds; they totter and stagger to the dead pile, where they put what was once a good-looking young man, then step back from the thickest of the stench to rest. The young Georgians approach, the goods on both sides are priced; the horn of soft soap, gets that fine double heart ring, a stick of wood is exchanged for a bone ring which cost a week of patient carving. A young Georgian now wants some of "'em er buttons with a chicken on 'em," and a couple of eagle buttons go for a twist of tobacco. The guard calls out: "Git in thar-r-now! we-kant-have-too many-a-youn's outen thar to wonst." They would not allow more than six or eight outside the gate at one time.

One day a prisoner by the name of John L. Ransom, being outside of the gate, and too weak for his task, fainted, not recovering soon, the Rebels thought him dead, and chucked him in the dead pile, where after lying in the hot sun for some time, he came to, sat up, and said, "For God sake! give me some water;" a Rebel officer looked at him

. a puzzled way, and said, "Lookey heah, Yank, if you hain't dead yet, you get back inside to die and thet putty darned quick." (John is alive yet and is the author of Andersonville Diary). I have no doubt that men were hauled to the trenches and buried who were not yet dead.

Sometimes the Rebel soldiers, for a consideration from the prisoners, would get permission to take a squad of them to the woods for fuel. This was working nicely and we were getting a supply of wood through that source, until some of the prisoners abused the privilege by tying their guards up to trees and running away, which stopped the going out for wood. When going to the woods in this manner we filled our stomach with leaves and weeds, in order to get something green. We had a craving desire for onions, potatoes, pickles, meat and salt, none of which we had for months; any green substance would be eagerly devoured. *Our* mess had a stalk of green corn, about knee high, growing by our sleeping ground, and guarded it as though it were gold. A crazy fellow came along one day, snatched the stalk, and ran away into the crowd, eating at it as fast as he could, destroying our summer's crop.

The crowd was growing denser every day, the rations less, and water worse, the sun poured down with almost tropical heat. "The tender skinned blondes burned in blisters, which soon made sores for the maggot flies to breed in." The great heat of the sun was reducing the quantity of water in the creek; we had dug some wells, but they soon became so filthy the water could not be used. The side hill of sandy ground above these wells, and, in fact, the whole pen, had been completely honey-combed, with small round holes, as deep as the arm would reach, which were used for the purpose of nature; these holes soon became alive with maggots, and a shower of rain filled them until the mass flowed over the surface and leached into the wells. The human filth had accumulated and stopped the passage of water through the stockade; it backed slowly, and spread this mass of filth out over the quagmire and on to the low ground occupied by some of the prisoners.

About this time John H. Winder gets a dispatch from the Rebel War Department, asking: "Have you room for more prisoners?" Winder answered, "Yes, send them on. We are doing more for the Confederacy here, in getting rid of the Yanks, than twenty of Lee's best regiments at the front." Sherman sent a large force of cavalry to release us; when Winder heard they were coming he issued an order to the commander of the artillery to be ready, and when the Yankee cavalry got within seven miles of the pen, to open fire on the prisoners with grape and canister and continue the firing, as long as a prisoner lived; but our cavalry was defeated, and part of them captured and turned in the pen with us.

Colonel C. T. Chandler, of the Confederate army was sent by Jefferson Davis, to inspect the Andersonville prison. He performed his duties carefully, and in his report to Davis, he says: "I called the attention of Captain Wirz and General Winder to the frightful mortality that must certainly follow the crowded and filthy condition of the prison, and pointed to them how this could easily be remedied; and I recommended a change in diet, from corn-meal to one of vegetables, which were quite plenty in the surrounding country." To all of which Winder indifferently replied: "The present arrangement is good enough, as it is having the desired effect, and if let alone will soon thin the prisoners out so there will be plenty of room." Col. Chandler hastened to Richmond, made his report and recommended an immediate change in the officers of the prison. The result was, Jefferson Davis *promoted* John H. Winder to general in command of all the prisons in the Confederacy. Who will say, with any pretense at telling the truth, that Jeff Davis is not a murderer? Where is there a man in existence, who has such a pile of *murder* and *brutality* unloaded at his door? That thousands of murders committed on helpless captives, in the Confederacy, were done with his full knowledge and permission, there is not one shadow of doubt, and which we only need use the Confederate evidence and records to prove; and say nothing of the *fourteen thousand graves at Andersonville, that harvest of death*, reaped from twelve acres of ground in less than one year and nearly four thousand of that number in one single month.

CHAPTER IV.

Time Drags Slowly.—Pastimes.—The "Races."—Stockade Enlarged..—Only Seventeen Hundred to the Acre.—A Providential Flood.—"Death's Acre."—Two Guards Voice their Opinions.—The Miraculous Spring.—Heartlessness of Church People.—Father Hamilton, a True Christian.—Another Promise of Exchange Only a Ruse to get us to Charleston, S. C.—I Escape from the Train, but Voluntarily Return.—Better Rations and Kinder-hearted People at Charleston.—One Southern Lady Arrested for Giving a Basket of Bread to "Yanks."—Sisters of Charity.—Taken to Florence, S. C.—A Second Edition of "Worse than Hell on Earth."—Twelve Thousand Men on Seven Acres.—The "Hospital."—Flanking for Rations.—Barrett, the Demon.—Starving Us.—Eating Raw Rice.—Its Terrible Effects.—Whipping Men to Death.—The Brute Still Living at Augusta, Ga.—Insanity.—Hands and Feet Drop off the Living Skeletons.—John W. January and Others Amputate Their Own Feet.—About Three Hundred Join the Confederacy.—Language Inadequate to Depict the Horrors of this Awful Prison.

Time was moving slowly; it seemed like the sun was weeks in crossing the sky of polished steel, and we were rapidly sinking into depravity. We had told all the stories we knew and heard all our neighbors knew. Every scrap of reading matter was worn out. There were yet a few cards and checkerboards in use. Some amusement was had from louse-racing; one way of racing graybacks was to lay a tin-plate or half-canteen in the sun until hot, then drop on the racers and bet on your favorite running off the plate first. Sometimes fights occurred over these races. A day's rations would be staked, and the interest became as great as though thousands of dollars were staked in these plentiful times. The favorite graybacks which had won a number of races for the men they had boarded with, would now be pitted, and on them depended a feast or a famine. A crowd of coolly dressed gentlemen gather round, giving and taking side bets, offering to bet that they have a louse that can beat any grayback in the crowd. The half-canteen is ready, the racers are held over it, at the word "go" they drop to the heated tin and strike out for a cooler place; one is rapidly nearing the edge, he suddenly turns in another direction. His master looks wicked and accuses his opponent, saying: "You blowed my louse!" The lie passes, there is a tumble in which a dozen take a hand, and which all amounts to a few bitten fingers and several dugouts smashed in. The race is a failure and the race stock lost in the filthy sand.

Men in our condition were sure to be peevish and irritable, and the best of friends would quarrel about a trifling matter. The light-weights would get on their feet, stagger around and balance in front of their opponent, stinging words would pass, then the bony fist launch feebly out, it misses its mark and its owner following, goes to the ground; the other fellow in trying to ward off the blow loses his balance and falls. This ends the fight as they are too much exhausted to renew it.

There are now *thirty-five-thousand* prisoners in the pen! Never before was there such a mass of humanity crowded on such a small and filthy place! We learn from the Rebel sergeants that there is an addition being built on the north end of the prison. We can hear the chopping and falling of timber and the peculiar singing of hundreds of slaves who are working on the addition to the prison. About the middle of July the guards are taken off the north stockade, openings are made in the wall and the prisoners who are located near the swamp are ordered to go to the new grounds.

The exodus begins, and what a sight! As they pass through the little lanes which we have opened for them their own mothers and wives would hardly own them. Some have lost all their teeth, hair, eye-brows and beard, some are rotten and full of squirming worms, others have their finger and toe-nails sloughed off. All this is the effect of slow starvation, sameness of food, over-crowding and filth. They look as if there was not flesh enough on a thousand of them to feed a small flock of crows; those who are able to walk are helping their comrades along— all excited with new hope that they may yet live to see the old flag and the loved ones at home.

The new addition increased the size of the pen to nearly twenty acres, which greatly relieved the crowded condition of the prisoners; but yet, there were about seventeen hundred to the acre.

It was a great pleasure to get on the clean, sweet ground; every green weed and herb was plucked and devoured, the wood and stumps were gathered and stored for scarce times. In addition to being thus comforted we were now getting news from Sherman through the prisoners being brought in.

Early in August a heavy rain fell, it came down in torrents and suddenly raised the little creek, the water breaking away the stockade, swept through the prison and opened a large space in the palisades where it passed out. The Rebels soon had a large force guarding the gap. The flood pretty thoroughly cleaned the swamp; our police organization got permission to send men out on parole and procure lumber with which a sluice was made nearly the whole length of the creek through the pen. Through this long box or sluice the creek ran with a tolerable current; all the prisoners who were able to get to this had to

use it as a sink, but there were many who were crippled with scurvy
and had lost all their immediate comrades by death. In order to get
water, these men would crawl down to some low, filthy ground near the
creek. We called this ground "death's acre," for here could be seen more
dead and dying than at any other place in the pen. Here would accu-
mulate the remnants of messes. There would be from fifty to a
hundred who had been active young and middle-aged men from loving
Northern homes, clinging to the last spark of life, wallowing in their own
filth, many of them reduced to idiocy and some could not speak; the
ground under them giving off the most suffocating stench to mingle with
that of bodies decaying in the hot sun. Sometimes we would go and
carry them water, of which they would drink largely but the stench
driving us away before we could serve all, they would stretch out their
wasted hands and implore us by words and signs to give them water,
the glassy look of their eyes telling us they would soon be out of
misery, we leave them to die. We have all the sick comrades we can see
to on our own ground, and we must not neglect them for those we can
not save with the means at hand.

One of the guard, noticing a neighboring guard looking at the sights
on "death's acre," said: "Jeems, thet's hell, ain't it? Don't yer reckon
they wush't thay'd staid to hum an' not tried whooping we 'uns? I'll
bet ef tha dose eny of 'em git outen thar, thay'll have sense 'nuff to
stay to hum, an' when these'ens tells them'ens up no'th what dey kotch
down heah, tha'll all stay to hum too; Old Windah knows what he's
doin', you ken bet yer recken?" "Yes, but," says James, "thet ar's
too darn'd bad, thar's lots o' clean places out hyar that 'em ere sick uns
mout be put on to, and the folks round about yar would give 'em taters

an' truck, an' lots of 'em would get well; I couldn't use a dog that-awa."
"Neither could I use a dog thet a 'way, but these fellers hain't half ez
good ez dogs; didn't you heer Giner'l Cobb say when he was a talkin',
thet they was a set o' thieves, fightin' fur thet ole niggah Lincoln?
Darn a cuss thet'll fite fur a niggah, d'orter rot; they killed my brother
up to Atlanta, an' hit'll take a big passel of 'um to pay fur him, an' I'm
gwine to kill all on um I ken."

One morning about the middle of August we noticed a long skinny
prisoner hurrying to his mud dugout and calling to his messmates said:
" Hurry up, hand me the boot-leg bucket! There is a spring of just
bully good water bursted out, up by the "dead-line" north of the
creek, and there is a big crowd there, but I think I can get some of the
water." We followed him near to the "dead-line," about half-way
between the creek and the north gate, and there, just beyond the "dead-
line" was a large vein of water running out of the ground; some of the
prisoners had tied cups and cans on sticks and were dipping the *clean,
fresh water* and giving it to those around to drink. The prisoners jammed
around until several are shot for crowding the "dead-line," then the chief
of our police comes and takes possession of the grounds. The spring
is led some distance inside the "dead-line," one of our police guards are
stationed over it and all have to take turns to get water. At times,
there would be over a thousand men in line, as you see at the general
delivery in a city post-office.

After this several springs appeared in different places in the pen near
the swamp and the health of the prison began to improve; but those
who had been poisoned by the damnable stuff we had been drinking
were dying like rotton sheep. " The churches of all denominations,

except one solitary Catholic priest, (Father Hamilton), ignored us as wholly as they would dumb beasts." Father Hamilton was the only religious minister that I ever knew to come into the prison at Andersonville, and I certainly believe he was a true Christian; he would minister to the Catholic and Protestant alike. Rebel Masons interested themselves in assisting their brother Masons in presents of medicine, food, tent material, reading and writing material, vegetables and in many ways not known to those not familiar with Masonry. I was neither a Catholic nor a Mason, but I do want to give credit to every merciful act shown in that hell; they were so few that it takes but little space to give them. Some of the Confederate doctors were kindhearted and shed tears over our distress, but they were powerless to give relief under the management of Jefferson Davis and his assistants, Winder and Wirz.

After the fall of Atlanta, the Rebels becoming fearful that so large a number of us together might cause our army to make an invasion for our release, concluded to send part of us to some other part of the Confederacy. They got off the exchange-news dodge, in order to keep us from trying to escape while in transit. They circulated the report that the commissioners of exchange had met and were about to agree on a general exchange of all prisoners. Early in September, a Confederate officer came inside and calling all the sergeants of detachments together, he said: "Prisoners, I am instructed by General Winder to tell you that a general exchange of prisoners has been agreed upon; your vessels are now waiting for you at Savannah and Charleston. Detachments, from one to ten, will leave to-morrow morning." This news spread rapidly through the pen, some wept for joy, the cripples seemed to take new life and all was excitement. Some, who had not walked for weeks, got on their feet, filled with new hope. We were taken out and put on the cars, the rebels acting as if they did not care whether we ran away or not. The car doors were left open, a guard sat carelessly in the door. We are surely going to our lines this time. We are told that our train-load goes to Charleston, S. C. Night comes on, the guard in our car door goes to sleep; the fresh, sweet air from the woods makes me feel like I mightbe able to walk; perhaps the Rebels are fooling us again; the train stops, waiting for another train to pass.

We are on a side-track by a long cotton platform; I look out, the guard still sleeps, I take the cap from his gun and slip quietly under the cotton platform; I am alone; the nearest point to our army is over two hundred miles; in my condition I cannot make five miles a night; it may be that the exchange is all right, and the boys will be at their homes or with their regiments, while I am sick and friendless in an enemy's country. I hear an engine whistle and the rumbling of the train we are waiting for. What had I better do, lie still, or go with the boys? The bell of our engine rings, I crawl back in the car, and many times did I curse myself for it afterward. In time we arrived at Charleston, and found the exchange a delusion; we were put in the large jail-yard and kept for a few days, then moved to the outer edge of town to the race-tracks. Here we had fresh, clean ground and our rations were better, the people seemed kind-hearted and would have done much for our relief if our keepers had allowed them. Ladies came with baskets of bread and asked permission to give it to the prisoners; one lady, on being refused, threw loaf by loaf over the line until her basket was empty. She was arrested as a "Yankee sympathizer." The Sisters of Charity come with clothing and medicines and asked in the name of mercy to be allowed to help the suffering. They give out that which they have with them, but are told that if they have any more to give to the Confederate needy.

About one hundred of our comrades were taken forcibly and put to work throwing up Rebel breastworks on Sullivan's Island. The Union batteries, supposing them Rebels, shell them and several are killed and many wounded before it is found out they are Union prisoners. The Rebels   brought back those who were not killed and laughed at the joke they had played on the "Yanks." We staid at Charleston until about the middle of October; during this time many fires occurred from the shells thrown from our batteries into the city.

We were again loaded on the cars, and this time sent to Florence, S. C. Here we found another stockade, though much smaller than the one at Andersonville. The walls were about sixteen feet high, the earth banked nearly to the top of the wall on the outside; this came from a deep wide ditch, which it was thought would prevent tunneling. The "dead-line" here was marked out by a little ditch which only ran part way round the wall. The balance of the line was just where the guards chose to claim it. They differed as to its location, and many prisoners lost their lives because of this difference of opinion. A small creek, running from north to south, through the center of the pen, furnished the water. There were about eight thousand prisoners in the pen when we arrived. The tops and refuse of the trees from which the stockade timbers were cut were left on the ground. From these the prisoners had constructed huts and dugouts. Some were too sick and weak to make anything but a hole in the ground big enough to back into, and some did not have this much. Frequently some of these mud dens would cave in on the occupants, and they would be smothered; if this happened in the night their cries and moans would go unheeded, so common were the cries of distress and misery. There never was a moment in the day or night that we were free from the cries of agony. The building material was all used up when we arrived, and we resorted to mud brick, but the rainy season was now coming on and our houses, or kind of bee-hives, would only stand between showers. We had about seven acres of available ground, and there were twelve thousand of us to occupy it. I was sergeant of the 12th thousand, the greater part of whom were sick men, who had to be counted where they lay. As there were a number of dead and dying every morning I would have as many of them counted as I could persuade the Rebel sergeant to believe could eat their rations; I played a number of dead men on him at different times. The counting would be done in the morning, and the rations come in in the afternoon; this would leave on my hands the rations of eight or ten men, who died between counting and issuing time, and I got an extra ration for the duties of sergeant of a thousand. By this I had enough to eat and some to spare for my less fortunate comrades. Our police got permission from the prison commander and a number of prisoners were put on parole of honor to go outside and get material to construct some sheds, to put the sick under. The northwest corner of the pen was cleared of the prisoners' dugouts, rude sheds were constructed, a police guard put around this space, and it was called the "Hospital." The sick were carried in and laid in two double rows under each shed; each double row was called a ward. A little path was left between the feet of the row on either side, so the attendants could give them attention. This arrangement of the sick broke up my thousand. I had no means now of getting extra rations, and I began to lose flesh again. I tried what we called "flanking" for rations. This was done by being counted in several different thousands. As soon as I was numbered in the thousand I belonged to I would slip over to a thousand which was not yet counted, stand in line and be listed there, thus getting two rations, or rather beating the Rebels out of one ration. This became practiced by so many that the prison commander (Lieutenant Barrett, of the 5th Georgia) caught one man and ordered him to be stripped of his clothes; he then tied him over a barrel, and, with a leather whip with five or six hard lashes (called the "cat), he cut the miserable man's back into shreds, and he was dead before they got him untied. Barrett then swore that he was going to do every one who was playing that game just as he did this man. He ordered the thousand to all fall in line and made them go to the east side of the small creek, intending to count them as they recrossed, but his counting qualities were so bad that he got puzzled before the first thousand was half over, so he gave it up for that day, saying he would take another day for it. Barrett was the most brutal fool I ever met. On the least provocation he would become so enraged that he would stamp and swear at everybody near him.

About this time he discovered some freshly dug earth near the creek, he swore there was a tunnel being dug some place and he intended to find it or starve the whole camp to death. He notified us that when we would surrender those tunnel-workers he would issue rations, and not before. That day passed away and no rations came in; the second

THE HOSPITAL SHED AT FLORENCE.

came and went the same, men were dying like starved sheep. The poor fellows would go to the creek and drink as full of water as they could hold, trying to keep their stomachs filled to prevent the grinding pain that only those have felt who have gone four and five days without food. The third day four men volunteered to start a sham tunnel and own it, to satisfy the cowardly fool, reasoning that it was better for a few to suffer punishment than to starve all to death.

These brave fellows acknowledged that they had started a tunnel. Barrett put them in irons, saying to them with an oath, " I appoint to-morrow as a day on which you will remember me." He then caused to be issued two-thirds of a pint of raw rice to each man, many of the prisoners having no fuel or means of cooking, ate their share raw; some were not able to chew the hard grains, their teeth being lost from scurvy. The scene that followed can not be described. In the course of several hours, many who had ravenously devoured the raw rice, were suffering and dying in all the agonies of cramp colic. Barrett stood on top of the gate, gleefully looking at the scene, saying: " I'll learn you to look out for these fellows that is trying to dig outen here, and tell me in time or I'll starve the last d—d one of you to death; you can't fool with me, I'm h—l when I start, you'll find out." This starving strain on the weakened constitutions of the prisoners carried them off in large numbers. The next morning, Barrett, after hardening his heart with villainous whiskey, brought out our comrades to be tortured for something they were not guilty of. Their hands were tied behind their backs, a small rope drawn tightly around each thumb, the rope then passed over a log, the ends of which rested on two cabins occupied by the Rebel officer. Barrett and his assistants pull on the rope until the victims are raised from the ground, thus twisting the muscles of the arms and shoulders producing the most terrible agony. The poor fellows screamed with pain and begged the guards "for God's sake, to shoot them," Barrett all the while showering from his tongue the most bitter invectives he could master. After a time, three faint away, and their heads hang limply forward, the fourth sets his teeth hard together, his muscles contracted and his body and face take on a horribly set appearance.

When Barrett is satisfied the men are taken down; one is dead, two recover and the other is incurable with lock-jaw, from which he died next day. The two who recover are turned into the pen and given some corn-meal, the first they had eaten for nearly four days. All this is done under the eyes of John H. Winder, Jeff. Davis' friend and counselor. Barrett was a low, ill-born wretch of the most brutal type. He seemed to delight in being present when a slave was to be tied up by the thumbs and whipped, and he took pride in showing the guards how he could knock down and kick the poor helpless imbecile prisoners, who were so idiotic that they could not understand him, and would stand and stare vacantly when he spoke to them. He practiced the most brutal and barbarous cruelties on this class of helpless prisoners. Barrett continued in command of the interior of the prison until in March, when the few survivors of his cruelty were sent to our lines. We never knew what became of Barrett until about two years ago a comrade living at Augusta, Ga., stated through the *National Tribune* that Barrett was living at that place. How such a murderer can go unpunished is more than we can understand. If one of us, who suffered worse than death at his hands, should happen to come into

HUNG UP BY THE THUMBS TO ONE OF THE REBEL CABINS FOR TRYING TO ESCAPE.

his presence, and Barrett should suddenly take the lock-jaw, and die, we would be hunted to the end of the earth and executed as a murderer. A large number of those who had been in prison over a year were now insane. They seemed to lose all power of speech and memory; they could not tell their own names and did not know whether they had been in prison a day or six years. If spoken to, their only answer would be a far-away look as if they were trying to recall something beyond the reach of their memory. They wandered aimlessly about and kept their comrades constantly watching to keep them from the "dead-line." As the winter weather grew colder, many of those who kept their mind and speech, now found that their extremities were dead, hands and feet would come off with a dry rot or what was termed gangrene; most of these cases were in the hospital, in which I now was wardmaster of the second ward. Sometimes the leg would be sensible to near the ankle, the skin and spongy bones of the joints decayed, leaving the sinews holding the foot or hand to the leg or arm. We would take a pair of scissors or an old razor and cut the sinews, removing the useless hand or foot. This was done with but little pain to the patients. Some of the patients would lay for a week, apparently dead, but could answer when spoken to; there was no pulse in the wrist, but a faint tremble could be felt over the heart. All these patients were destitute of flesh, there being nothing but the sinew and skin, stretched over a frame of bones. I never heard any name for this disease, but I knew it was the closing scene of a lingering starvation. Some of these poor fellows would cut off their own feet and seemed determined to live. Comrade John W. January, who now lives at Minonk, Ill., being one of the number who amputated his own feet. The Rebels were now trying in

every way to get our men to enlist, offering clothing, money and plenty
to eat. A few of the prisoners went out and enlisted with the view of
trying to escape to our lines at the first opportunity, which, of course,
the Rebels watched to see that no such chances were given; and then,
there were our old Andersonville pests, the "Raiders," they went out ·
and enlisted. They did not care if the Rebels did destroy the government. It was anything with them to get out of that hell. In all,
there were, perhaps, three hundred who joined the Rebels, the balance
of us only set our determination to stand more firmly by the old flag.
Tehse men who went out dressed in Rebel uniform and after a few days
were marched through the prison carying Rebel guns and the Rebel
flag and inviting their former comrades to join them; we told them we
woul l starve and rot the balance of our lives before we would carry a
gun under that Rebel "rag." We all had the most utter contempt fo:
anyone who would do or say anything to help the Rebels. I will not
attempt to tell the horrors of this Florence prison, only, I will say, that
the human misery was greater than at Andersonville. Many were
murdered at the "dead-line;" the gangrene was terrible and many died
from sheer starvation.

CHAPTER V.

The winter wore away, during which many perished from cold and wet. Early in February, Sherman was getting so close that the Rebels sent all the prisoners who could walk or stand on their feet to Goldsborough, N. C. We of the hospital squad staid with the sick and gathered from in the prison all the sick we could put under the sheds, and arranged the balance so we could give them water. They were decreasing rapidly by death. The Rebels told us if we would take an oath not to go beyond the stockade they would take off the guards; glad to get rid of these murderers, we consented; we were then sworn not to hold conversation with negroes or slaves, and not to go beyond the limits of the stockade; the nurses counseled together and agreed to stay with the sick, as it would not be long until our troops would release us. The temptation to run away was great, but considering the helplessness of our sick comrades, not a man of the nurses would say go. They were all kind-hearted men, who did all in their power for the suffering, wretched sick under those bleak leaky sheds at Florence, S. C.

One morning about the last of February, a Rebel officer came in and ordered us to get every man over to the railroad (about a quarter of a mile away), and they would take us to our lines. Some of the sick were taken in wagons; some crawled most of the distance. We took all but those thought to be dying; they were left without help of any kind; there were perhaps thirty or forty in this condition. We finally loaded the sick in freight cars, and started, running all that day and night, and about the middle of the second day our train stopped in the rear of a Rebel line of battle; the Rebels were all excitement, and soon ran our train back as fast as they could go; we would have jumped off and taken to the woods had it not been for our sick boys. In time the train stopped and we were ordered off the cars, and camped in the woods, which was a picnic for us; but the Rebels acted like they expected an attack. Some Rebel cavalry helped them guard us that night, and next day we were sent back to our old quarters at Florence. This discouraged our sick, but we cheered them up and told them that the "Salvation of the Lord was close at hand, and the Confederacy was bursted."

We found some of those who were dying when we left, four days before were still alive. We wet their lips with water, and fixed them as comfortably as we could. Some whom we took with us died, and we left them near the railroad for the section men to bury. About the 1st of March we were ordered to the road again; we worked our sick aboard the cars and started over the same road; we knew now that our forces had captured Wilmington; we ran along without adventure; sometimes when the train would make a short stop we would take out our dead and lay them beside the track; we were going in the direction of Wilmington; our engine carried a white flag. We were in suspense to know what was going to be done with us. After awhile some of the boys said: "Hello! there's a blue-coat!" We looked; sure enough, there are several blue-coats out foraging. Peeping out the door we see bright guns flashing in the sunlight, and soon make out that it is a line of Union pickets.

The sick crawl to the door and look out. The guards offer no objection, but look badly scared. Our train moves up with the engine through the line of pickets. The Rebel officer in charge of us salutes a Union major. They talk a moment and the major signals a Union officer at the picket line, who advances with about thirty unarmed men, and several surgeons. The Rebel guards now move a few yards away and look ashamed, and sneaking. There is not a word exchanged between them and our men; our Union friends now come up to the cars, and kindly help the sick out; the Union soldiers helping are wiping their eyes; others are setting their teeth hard and casting wicked glances at the Rebels; but there is the flag of truce; that must be respected, and they cannot express their thoughts. A Union soldier comes up and asks if there is a man with us by the name of Wilcox. A sick man recognizes the speaker, and says: "That's your brother," pointing to one of the unfortunates whose mind is gone. He does not know his own name when called by his brother. All this does not affect us, we have seen nothing but misery for a year and a half, and it seems strange to see people weep when we are so full of joy. We try to sing "Home at last from a foreign shore;" but the voices are weak and break down.

We went through the line of guards to the edge of the woods, where the kind soldiers built up big fires, and did everything in their power to make us comfortable. They divided their clothing, giving us shirts, stockings, and everything they could possibly spare. Wilmington was more than a mile away; these troops were on picket, being part of Schofield's corps. They were as noble-hearted, fine-looking soldiers as I ever saw. Our forces had been in possession of Wilmington but a short time, and they were not prepared to receive and clothe us. Some wagons came over from Wilmington loaded with rations, camp-kettles were put on the fire and coffee made, boxes were bursted open, and crackers given out, and vinegar and onions, all of which many of us had not tasted for eighteen months. Our surgeons looked after those who did not seem to have judgment, and warned them not to eat too much; they said we could drink all the coffee we wanted; and some drank until they seemed intoxicated. The surgeons took charge of the sick, whose numbers were being rapidly reduced by death. Next morning we got some soap from the soldiers and a number of us went to a little creek near by and washed off as much prison filth as we could scour loose. We ate a hearty breakfast, and all who were able to walk marched over to Wilmington, our boys yelling themselves hoarse when we sighted the old stars and stripes floating from a steeple over in Wilmington. We felt that we were in *God's country at last.* It seemed as if we had been gone from it for twenty years or more, and it seems now, in looking back, that it can not be possible that we did pass through those awful hells; we do not wonder that so many died, but we do wonder how any lived to look back at the broad trial of death, which strewed our way with the bones of those true and brave comrades, whose memories we will ever cherish as martyrs to our country's cause.

But we point with pride to those sixty thousand graves, and say, these comrades chose the most cruel death rather than dishonor their country by in any way assisting its enemies to destroy it. Under the most trying circumstances, naked, starving, and racked with pain and disease, with certain torture and death staring them in the face, did they refuse the oft repeated offers of relief, of enlisting in the Rebel army, or working in their shops. These *sixty thousand* young men gave up all their bright hopes and prospects of loving homes and pursuits of happiness and submitted to cruel torture and death, believing that their sacrifices and deeds of heroism, would ever be kept fresh in the memory of those who would enjoy the freedom for which this price was paid. But to-day we have many ungrateful people who clamor to suppress the recital of these comrades' suffering, claiming that it will only breed sectional hatred, and that these stories are written and told in a spirit of animosity. To which I will say, I know that the truths written and told of these prison hells are very unwelcome to this class of people; but remember, we do not hold the masses of the people, or soldiers of the South responsible for the brutal murders of our fellow-prisoners, and for all these misguided people, we hold the greatest respect, except for those who admire and applaud those bold bad men who wantonly and premeditatedly did murder their helpless captives. Again we are told that Jeff Davis and his officers did not have the provisions to feed their captives. This excuse was removed by our government offering to furnish food, clothes and medicines, which was refused. We know that they had no excuse for denying us pure air, water, room, and the means of constructing shelter.

We begged and pleaded with tears in our eyes that we be per-

mitted to save our lives by ditching and draining out the swamps in
Andersonville, and getting material from the adjoining pine forest to
shelter us from sun and rain.   To those who say Jeff and his cabinet
did not murder their captives, we ask them to discard *all* testimony of
Union soldiers, and take the evidence of Southern people and the
Confederate war records.   Examine the reports of Confederate surgeons, appointed to inspect the prisons, and you will see where they ·
hasten back to Davis and report to him the horrible condition of the
prisons and the useless destruction of life there—see where they
recommend the immediate removal of the inhuman keepers, and the
appointment of humane keepers in their stead.   You will see that Davis
did nothing of the kind, but he did *promote John H. Winder* to
the command of all the prisons in the South, with full power to torture
and murder as he pleased, and, when you have examined all this calmly,
if you have one spark of humanity in your soul, you will never express
your admiration for that perjured murderer and his traitorous advisers
who "dragged eleven millions of people into war, against which their
souls revolted." Occasionally we hear it said that the Southern
prisoners were treated as badly in the Northern prisons.   (This we never
hear from those who were confined in the Northern prisons).   The
graves under the lonely pines near the sites of those Southern prisons,
tell a story that cannot be disputed; there were but few of the Southern
prisons where a record was kept of the deaths, and where kept, it was
very imperfect; in the North there was a very complete record kept
and the deaths all reported.   Now the Rebel sympathizers claim that
the war records show a greater per cent. of deaths in Northern than in
Southern prisons, knowing full well that there never was one-fourth of

CAPT. WIRZ STAMPING TO DEATH SERGEANT S. H. NELSON, OF CO. I, 4TH VERMONT, DEC. 13, 1864. NO. OF GRAVE 12,283. THIS WAS ONE OF THE MANY CASES OF MURDER FOR WHICH WIRZ WAS TRIED AND HUNG IN NOVEMBER, 1865.

the mortality in the Southern prisons reported. The Confederate records show that they captured 188,145, and that they paroled or exchanged 94,073, leaving a balance of 94,072 to be accounted for; now give them credit for 10,000 who escaped or went into the Rebel army, what became of the remainder, the 84,072? *They perished in those prison hells*, or were pursued through fen and forest by blood-hounds and demons and their mangled corpses left to the carrion birds. Any of my comrades who were prisoners can bear witness to numbers who escaped and were never afterward heard of. I do not believe that more than one of every fifty who escaped ever reached the friendly shelter of the stars and stripes.

There were more Union soldiers lost their lives by the Southern prisons than were killed in the two thousand two hundred and sixty-one battles of the Rebellion. I am often asked the question: "Why did not our government exchange prisoners or send an army down there and release you?" The answer is: The Rebels demanded an exchange of man for man as far as they would go (except the negroes), and the excess to be paroled, which would release all white prisoners from confinement. Had this been done, Sherman would not have marched through Georgia, nor Grant have taken Richmond for at least one or two years more. For this reason: Out of the ninety-four thousand held by the Rebels, the Union army would not have got over twenty thousand fighting men, while on the other hand the North held two hundred and twenty-seven thousand of the best material of the Southern army, which nearly all to a man regardless of their paroles, would have been put against Grant and Sherman, and to have met and dislodged these old Confederate soldiers from their position of defense, our government would have been compelled to call out at least four hundred thousand fresh troops. This was the best terms the Rebels offered, except, at very near the close of the war they would have exchanged on most any terms; but our troops were releasing us, so the Rebels had to parole us and turn us over to our men. Now, as to sending an army to release us; does it ever occur to the questioner that we were generally kept in the most secure part of the South, and as remote from our army as possible? and that it was about as difficult for our troops to release us as it would have been for the Rebels to have marched to Chicago and freed the Rebel prisoners confined there. I do not find fault with the government for any apparent neglect; but I do think we ought to be remembered as being largely instrumental in bringing the war to a speedy termination.

I have passed over this picture rapidly, giving but a hasty outline of a text, which, were I to write as my memory sees it, I could fill a volume as large as the Bible. My object being to make a cheap pamphlet, I was limited in space, and consequently pruned the discription as much as possible; not even mentioning the names of true and noble men who passed through that awful test of patriotism—men who were my constant comrades, and who I have seen endure the most terrible pangs of starvation, their shrunken almost naked frames shivering with cold and wet, and faces pinched with pain and hunger; I have seen them offered food and comfort if they would join the Rebels; but gathering their filthy rags close about their shivering bodies they scornfully replied: "You can do your worst, we will never go back on the old stars and stripes." Reader, did these men join the Uuion army through patriotism? or was it for the thirteen dollars per month as is asserted by some of the renegade editors who justify the pension vetoes and returning the Rebel flags? I have no doubt that if the ingrates who make such assertions had been with us they would have either joined the Rebels or been hung, as were the six "Raiders," for robbing starving men of their food and clothing.

The principal part of the following I take from "Smith's Knapsack of Facts and Figures from '61 to '65:"

In the war for the preservation of the Union there were 2,261 battles fought:

Killed in battle............................... 44,238.
Died of wounds............................... 49,205.
" " disease............................ 186,216.
Died of unknown causes...................... 24,184.
Suicide, homicide and executions............ 526.
                                             ─────────
                                Total, 304,369.

Of this number 188,353 died in the hospitals. The loss of life of both North and South is estimated at 1,000,000. The debt and loss of the U. S., over $6,000,000,000.

There were sixteen Rebel prisons, where by counting the graves where grave-stones are erected, we find 36,401 graves of Union soldiers who died in prison. 11,599 of those released from prison died before reaching their homes; and soon after 12,000 of those who did reach their homes died, making 60,000 accounted for as losing their lives by the Rebel prisons; but a large number have never been accounted for; but I feel certain that many of the last mentioned died by the fangs of the terrible blood-hounds.

THE MAN WHO WAS RESPONSIBLE FOR THE MURDER OF HIS CAPTIVES DISGRACING HIS FOLLOWERS BY TRYING TO REPRESENT HIMSELF AS BEING HIS OWN MOTHER-IN-LAW.

ADDITIONAL TESTIMONY.

Since the foregoing is in type, a worn pamphlet has been put in the hands of the writer. It is a collection of testimony taken by a commissioner whose duty, it appears, was to inquire into the treatment of prisoners of war. It was published in November, '64, being long before the war closed, and while union prisoners were yet confined at Andersonville. We will add an extract from the testimony of one witness, who, through some favoritism was exchanged in August, '64, having been a prisoner a little less than two months. On arriving in our lines, he, with three comrades exchanged with him, went before President Lincoln and the commissioner, and under oath made a statement from which the following brief extract is taken :

The following statement was drawn up for the Commission, and sworn to by the parties signing it. They were exchanged on the 16th of August, and with three others were appointed by their companions in prison as a deputation to see President Lincoln in their behalf Deposition of PRIVATE TRACY:—

I am a private in the 82d New York Regiment of Volunteers, Company G. Was captured with about eight hundred Federal troops, in front of Petersburg, on the 22d of June, 1864. We were kept at Petersburg two days, at Richmond, Belle Isle, three days, then conveyed by rail to Lynchburg. Marched seventy-five miles to Danville, thence by rail to Andersonville, Georgia.

All blankets, haversacks, canteens, money, valuables of every kind, extra clothing, and in some cases the last shirt and drawers, had been previously taken from us.

On entering the Stockade Prison at Andersonville, we found it crowded with twenty-eight thousand of our fellow-soldiers. By *crowded*, I mean that it was difficult to move in any direction without jostling and being jostled. This prison is an open space, sloping on both sides, originally seventeen acres, now twenty-five acres, in the shape of a parallelogram, without trees or shelter of any kind. The soil is sand over a bottom of clay. The fence is made of upright trunks of trees, about twenty feet high, near the top of which are small platforms, where the guards are stationed. Twenty feet inside and parallel to the fence is a light railing, forming the "dead-line," beyond which the projection of a foot or finger is sure to bring the deadly bullet of the sentinel.

Through the ground, at nearly right-angles with the longer sides, runs or rather creeps a stream varying from five to six feet in width, the water about ankle deep, and near the middle of the enclosure, spreading out into a swamp of about six acres. Before entering this enclosure, the stream, or more properly sewer, passes through the camp of the guards, receiving from this source, and others farther up, a large amount of the vilest material, even the contents of the sink. The water is of a dark color, and an ordinary glass would collect a thick sediment. This was our only drinking and cooking water. It was our custom to filter it as best we could, through our remnants of haversacks, shirts and blouses. Wells had been dug, but the water proved so productive of diarrhœa that they were of no general use. The cook-house was situated on the stream just outside the stockade, and its refuse of decaying offal was thrown into the water. To these was added the daily large amount of base matter from the camp itself. One side of the swamp was naturally used as a sink, the men usually going out some distance into the water. Under the summer sun this place early became corruption too vile for description, the men breeding disgusting life, so that the surface of the water moved as with a gentle breeze.

The new-comers on reaching this would exclaim, "Is this hell?" yet they soon would become callous, and enter unmoved the horrible rottenness. The Rebel authorities never removed any filth. There was seldom any visitation by the officers in charge. Two surgeons were at one time sent by President Davis to inspect the camp, but a walk through a small section gave them all the information they desired, and we never saw them again.

Our only shelter from the sun and rain and night dews was what we could make by stretching over us our coats or scraps of blankets, which a few had, but generally there was no attempt by day or night to protect ourselves.

The clothing of the men was miserable in the extreme. Very few shoes of any kind, not two thousand had coats and pants, and those were late comers. More than one-half were indecently exposed, and many were naked.

The usual punishment was to place the men in the stocks, outside, near the Captain's quarters. If a man was missing at roll-call, the squad of ninety to which he belonged was deprived of the ration. The "dead-line" bullet, already referred to, spared no offender. One poor fellow, just from Sherman's army—his name was Roberts—was trying to wash his face near the "dead-line" railing, when he slipped on the clayey bottom, and fell with his head just outside the fatal border. We shouted to him, but it was too late.

The mental condition of a large portion of the men was melancholy, beginning in despondency and tending to a kind of stolid and idiotic indifference. Many spent much time in arousing and encouraging their fellows, but hundreds were lying about motionless, or stalking vacantly to and fro, quite beyond any help which could be given them within their prison walls. These cases were frequent among those who had been imprisoned but a short time.

Letters from home very seldom reached us, and few had any means of writing. In the early summer a large batch of letters—five thousand we were told—arrived, having been accumulating somewhere for many months. These were brought into camp by an officer, under orders to collect ten cents on each—of course most were returned, and we heard no more of them. One of my companions saw among them three from his parents, but he was unable to pay the charge.

Some few weeks before being released I was ordered to act as clerk in the hospital. This consists simply of a few scattered trees and fly tents, and is in charge of Dr. White, an excellent and considerate man, with very limited means, but doing all in his power for his patients.

The average of death through the earlier months was thirty a day; at the time I left the average was over one hundred and thirty, and one day the record showed one hundred and forty-six.

The proportion of deaths *from starvation*, not including those consequent on the diseases originating in the character and limited quantity of food, such as diarrhœa, dysentery and scurvy, I can not state; but to the best of my knowledge, information and belief, there were scores every month. We could, at any time, point out many for whom such a fate was inevitable, as they lay or feebly walked, mere skeletons, whose emaciation exceeded the examples given in Leslie's Illustrated for June 18, 1864. For example: in some cases the inner edges of the two bones of the arms, between the elbow and the wrist, with the intermediate blood vessels, were plainly visible when held toward the light. The ration, in quantity, was perhaps barely sufficient to sustain life, and the cases of starvation were generally those whose stomachs could not retain what had become entirely indigestible.

For a man to find, on waking, that his comrade by his side was dead, was an occurrence too common to be noted. I have seen death in almost all the forms of the hospital and battle-field, but the daily scenes in Camp Sumter exceeded in the extremity of misery all my previous experience.

The work of burial is performed by our own men, under guard and orders, twenty-five bodies being placed in a single pit, without head-boards, and the sad duty performed with indecent haste. Sometimes our men were rewarded for this work with a few sticks of firewood, and I have known them to quarrel over a dead body for the *job*.

Dr. White is able to give the patients a diet but little better than the prison rations—a little flour porridge, arrow-root, whiskey and wild or hog tomatoes. In the way of medicine, I saw nothing but camphor, whiskey and a decoction of some kind of bark—white oak, I think. He often expressed his regret that he had not more medicines. The limitation of military orders, under which the surgeon in charge was placed, s shown by the following occurrence: A supposed private, wounded in he thigh, was under treatment in the hospital, when it was discovered that he was a major of a colored regiment. The assistant surgeon, under whose immediate charge he was, proceeded at once not only to remove him, but to kick him out, and he was returned to the stockade, to shift for himself as well as he could. Dr. White could not or did not attempt to restore him.

After entering on my duties at the hospital, I was occasionally favored with double rations and some wild tomatoes. A few of our men succeeded, in spite of the closest examination of our clothes, in secreting some greenbacks, and with those were able to buy useful articles at exorbitant prices:—a tea-cup of flour at one dollar; eggs, three to six dollars a dozen; salt, four dollars a pound; molasses, thirty dollars a gallon; nigger beans, a small, inferior article (diet of the slaves and pigs, but highly relished by us), fifty cents a pint. These figures, multiplied by ten, will give very near the price in Confederate currency. Though the country abounded in pine and oak, sticks were sold to us at various prices, according to size.

Our men, especially the mechanics, were tempted with the offer of liberty and large wages to take the oath of allegiance to the Confederacy, but it was very rare that their patriotism, even under such a fiery trial, ever gave way. I carry this message from one of my companions to his mother: "My treatment here is killing me, mother, but I die cheerfully for my country."

Some attempts were made to escape, but wholly in vain, for, if the prison walls and guards were passed and the protecting woods reached, the bloodhounds were sure to find us out.

Tunneling was at once attempted on a large scale, but on the after-

announced to us that the plot was discovered, and from our huge pen we could see on the hill above us the regiments just arriving to strengthen the guard. We had been betrayed. It was our belief that spies were kept in the camp, which could very easily be done.

The number in camp when I left was nearly thirty-five thousand, and daily increasing. The number in hospital was about five thousand. I was exchanged at Port Royal Ferry, Aug. 16th, 1864.

PRESCOTT TRACY,
Eighty-second Regiment, N. Y. V.

City and County of New York, ss.

H. C. HIGGINSON and S. NOIROT, being duly sworn, say: That the above statement of Prescott Tracy, their fellow-prisoner, agrees with their own knowledge and experience.

H. C. HIGGINSON,
Co. K, Nineteenth Illinois Vols.
SILVESTER NOIROT,
Co. B, Fifth New Jersey Vols.

THE ANDERSONVILLE POSTOFFICE

By G. H. HOLLISTER, of Litchfield, Conn.

No blanket round his wasted limbs,
　Under the rainy sky he slept ;
While pointing his envenomed shafts,
　Around him Death, the archer, crept ;
He dreamed of hunger, and held out
　His hand to clutch a little bread,
That a white angel with a torch,
　Among the living and the dead,
Seemed bearing, smiling as he went ;
　The vision waked him, as he spied
The post-boy followed by a crowd
　Of famished prisoners, who cried
For letters—letters from their friends.
　Crawling upon his hands and knees
He hears his own name called, and lo !
　A letter from his wife he sees !

Gasping for breath, he shrieked aloud,
　And, lost in nature's blind eclipse,
Faltering amid the suppliant crowd,
　Caught it and pressed it to his lips.
A guard who followed, red and wroth,
　And flourishing a rusty brand,
Reviled him with a taunting oath,
　And snatched the letter from his hand.
" First pay the postage, whining wretch ! "
　Despair had made the prisoner brave,
" Then give me back my money, sir !
　I am a captive—not a slave !

(70)

You took my money and my clothes ;
   Take my life, too—but let me know
How Mary and the children are,
   And I will bless you ere I go."

The very moonlight through his hands
   As he stood supplicating, shone,
And his sharp features shaped themselves
   Into a prayer, and such a tone
Of anguish there was in his cry,
   For wife and children, that the guard—
Thinking upon his own—passed by,
   And left him swooning on the sward.
Beyond the " dead line " fell his head—
   The eager sentry knew his mark,
And with a crash the bullet sped
   Into his brain, and all was dark !
But when they turned his livid cheek
   Up toward the light, the pale lips smiled,
Kissing a picture fair and meek,
   That held in either hand a child.

DEATH-RATE AT ANDERSONVILLE.

From the Andersonville Death Register, as kept by the Rebels we find the deaths by states to be:

State	Deaths	State	Deaths
Alabama	15	New Jersey	170
Connecticut	315	New York	2,572
Delaware	45	North Carolina	17
Dist. of Columbia	14	Ohio	1,030
Illinois	350	Pennsylvania	1,811
Indiana	591	Rhode Island	74
Iowa	174	Tennessee	738
Kentucky	436	Vermont	212
Lousiana	1	Virginia	288
Maine	233	Wisconsin	244
Maryland	191	U. S. Army	399
Massachusetts	768	U. S. Navy	160
Minnesota	79	Citizens, teamsters, etc.	166
Michigan	630	Men that were hung	6
Missouri	97	Unknown Union soldiers	443
New Hampshire	124	Died with small-pox	68
		Total	12,912

The dead were not all recorded; there were 13,706 buried at Andersonville.

In August, one in eleven died!

In September, one in every three died!

In October, one in every two died!

In November, one in every three died!

Does the reader fully understand that in September one-third of those in the pen died; that in October one-half of the remainder perished, and in November one-third of those who still survived, died? Read this over carefully again, and it will remove all doubts as to the ability of the surviving prisoners to exaggerate those Hell-holes, that have never been surpassed for barbarism and cruelty.

Many people seem to regard the matter of having been a prisoner of war as merely an absence of freedom, a deprivation of the pleasures and excitements of ordinary life.

I will quote the language of one who was a prisoner in those awful hells. He says:

"Think of this death-life, month after month! Think of men of delicate organizations, accustomed to ease and luxury, of fine taste and passionate love for the beautiful, without a word of sympathy or a whisper of hope, wearing their days out amid such scenes. Not a pleasant sound, nor a sweet odor, nor a vision of fairness ever reached them. They were buried as completely as if they lay beneath the ruins of Pompeii or Herculaneum. They breathed mechanically, but were shut out from all that renders existence endurable. Every sense was shocked perpetually, and yet the heart, by a strange inconsistency, kept up its throbs, and preserved the physical being of a portion of those wretched captives, who no doubt often prayed to die.

"Take into consideration the scant and miserable rations that no one, unless he be half famished, can eat ; the necessity of going cold and hungry in the wet and wintry weather ; the constant torture of vermin which no care nor precaution can free one ; the total isolation ; the supreme dreariness, the dreadful monotony, the perpetual turning inward of the mind upon itself ; the self-devouring of the heart week after week and month after month."

Is it to be wondered at that the few survivors are mental and physical wrecks ?

IN THE SHADOW OF DEATH.

By J. H. GOODELL, M. D., Marseilles, Ill.

Go with me to yonder vale.
Can you hear that mournful wail?
Whence does it come? how can it be
That boasted Southern chivalry
Permits oppressions haughty power
To live in this, glad Freedom's hour?
Yet, still we hear it all around;
It even rises from the ground;
It's in the wind; it rides the gale;
It comes with rain, and goes with hail;
The insects tell it—not the birds.
For they are free as God's own words.
They only come just to the edge,
They will not look upon the page
Of the dark history written there,
The dev'lish acts, the gaunt despair
That made men imbecile while young,
By hellish acts thus to prolong
The life of that black Idol, grim,
Whose black, with its own blood, is dim,
Dim with the hearts and thraldom born,
Dim with the tears of children torn
From mother's breasts, a sad, sad throng
Crying to God, "how long! how long!"
Every nook within this vale
Re-echoes to this mournful tale.
"I died by slow starvation's stage,
When every moment was an age!
The little given me to eat,

At home I'd spurn beneath my feet.
It swarmed with vermine, big and ill,
Who, first of all, had had their fill,
Leaving behind their dead remains
A filthy mass; but made the gains,
Taking the sum of pris'ners fed,
A large amount as the year fled."
A little stream ran through the place,
In width about a soldier's pace;
A short distance, from the Stockade
Above, the Rebel camp was laid.
This stream ran through this camp and took
It's fill of filth from every nook,
So, when it came within "the pen"
For us to use, it represents
The sewage of five thousand men,
And cook-house slops, in its contents.
When the hot Sun of Summer came,
There rose a stench too vile to name;
So dense that you could see it rise
In festering fumes insult the skies.
Filth made the banks to this vile stream.
It never had the cheerful gleam
Which sparkles in the mountain brook
That from free air its sunshine took.
From out this poisoned slough we drank!
No wonder that our spirits sank,
No wonder that each lingering pain
Fanned old disease to life again.
Oh! I have not the words to tell
The dreadful horrors that befel
The soldier prisoned in this hell.
A few feet inward from the fence
That, twenty feet above the ground.
Ran the inclosure all around,

The dead line came, and the offense
Was death to him who ventured there,
The Rebel guard the arbiter.
One day I was with hunger crazed!
My mind, with all these sufferings, dazed!
I only cared to end it all
And put myself beyond the thrall
Of Davis and his Rebel crew,
Who could not on the battle plain,
With Southern chivalry's might and main,
Conquer the sturdy "Boys in Blue,"
But, sought this abject cowards way,
To starve out those he could not slay.
I ran, and on the dead line sank!
The boasting guard said "killed a Yank."

They ask us to forget the war!
All of these scenes to cover o'er!
To blot clear out from memory's page
And all this section strife assuage!
Can he who knows and hears to-day
Say to this page, "away! away!"?
Can he who looked upon this scene
With all its ghastly, filthy sheen,
Forget disease his body feels
As old age quicker on him steals?
Forget the misery untold?
Forget the boys who, stark and cold,
At mornings call were carried forth
And buried, not as at the North,
But drawn away, like hated things,
With jeers, and taunts, and cruel flings.

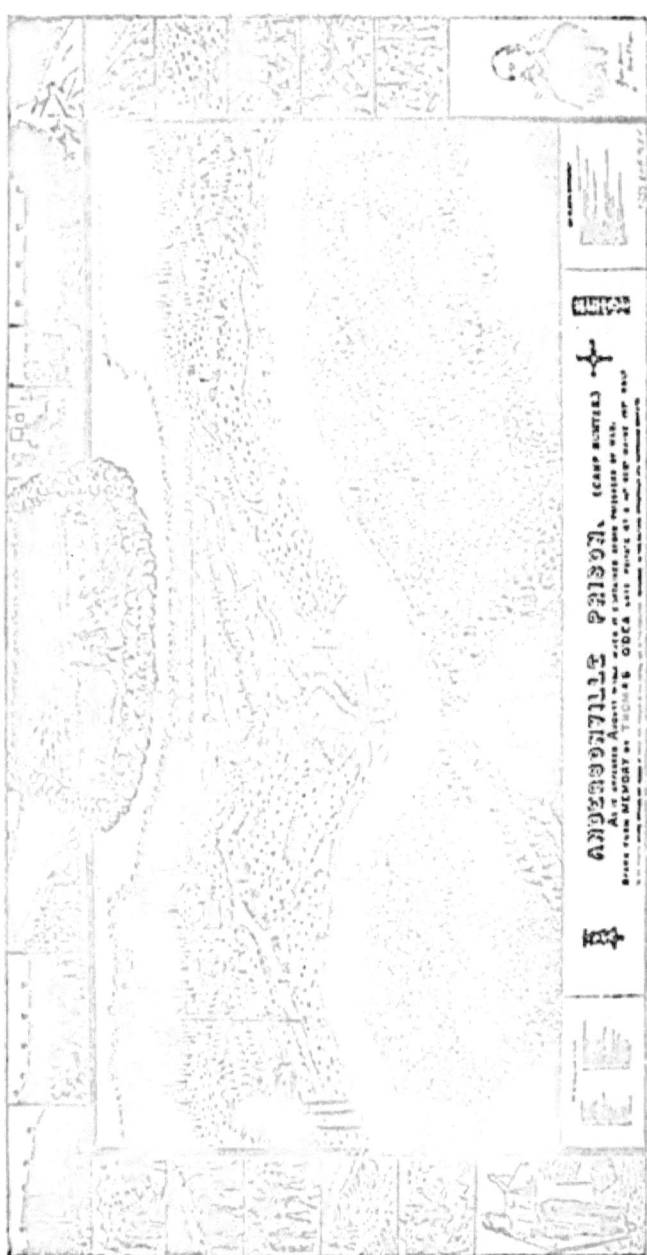

www.ingramcontent.com/pod-product-compliance
Lightning Source LLC
Chambersburg PA
CBHW020031030726
47499CB00007B/2375